FEAR OF THE GUEST

YIHAN SIM

Marshall Cavendish
Editions

© 2020 Marshall Cavendish International (Asia) Pte Ltd
Text © Sim Yi Han

Published by Marshall Cavendish Editions
An imprint of Marshall Cavendish International

A member of the
Times Publishing Group

Other Marshall Cavendish Offices:
Marshall Cavendish Corporation, 800 Westchester Ave, Suite N-641, Rye Brook,
NY 10573, USA • Marshall Cavendish International (Thailand) Co Ltd, 253 Asoke,
16th Floor, Sukhumvit 21 Road, Klongtoey Nua, Wattana, Bangkok 10110, Thailand •
Marshall Cavendish (Malaysia) Sdn Bhd, Times Subang, Lot 46, Subang Hi-Tech
Industrial Park, Batu Tiga, 40000 Shah Alam, Selangor Darul Ehsan, Malaysia

National Library Board, Singapore Cataloguing in Publication Data

Name(s): Sim, Yihan.
Title: Fear of the guest / Yihan Sim.
Description: Singapore : Marshall Cavendish Editions, [2020]
Identifier(s): OCN 1156324507 | ISBN 978-981-48-9313-8 (paperback)
Subject(s): LCSH: Good and evil--Fiction. | Ghost stories.
Classification: DDC S823--dc23

Printed in Singapore

Cover artwork by Dan Ng

Contents

客人来，看爸爸，
爸爸不在家，
我请客人先坐下，
再敬一杯茶。

When a guest comes, to see Papa,
but Papa is away,
"Please have a seat
and a cup of tea,"
this is what I must say.

– old nursery song

1

STRANGER IN THE DARK

A face in the window.

Its single luminous eye stared, wide and unblinking, beneath a swathe of long, black hair. Red, red lips curved upward lazily like the bow of a river *sampan* on moonlit waters.

Slowly, the face drew back and a slim white hand glided up, briskly sweeping the hair up into a tight, neat chignon, out of the eyes and snug at the nape of the neck. Lady Pontianak permitted herself a second to admire her reflection, patting her hair, pleased with herself. She had watched that YouTube tutorial four times to master the hairstyle.

Satisfied with her countenance, she turned away and surveyed the straggled group arrayed before her with a small sigh. The numbers dwindled slightly with every meeting. Most of its members did not look well; they were pale and faded around the edges.

The room they gathered in had seen better days. It was a silent, decaying flat; hollowed out and devoid of residents. The public housing block and its two neighbours had been drained of its inhabitants three years ago as a result of an en bloc sale. They stood patiently, gathering rust, mould and bird droppings, waiting to be demolished and turned into million-dollar condominiums more befitting of their gentrified neighbourhood.

Meanwhile, it served well as a meeting venue for the Grassroots Committee of Ghosts and Monsters. It was quiet and had plenty of space for the buffet catering. Or what passed for a buffet catering. Little chittering house spirits had generously brought the offerings they received that week, consisting of pears, oranges, pineapples, iced gem biscuits, and *huat kueh*, the steamed rice flour cakes that all ghosts loved. The meeting members had fruit punch in small white plastic cups, savouring it gleefully, pleased at how human they looked.

Lady Pontianak nodded at Uncle Bhuta, the Secretary for the Grassroots Committee of Ghosts and Monsters.

"Remember to take the attendance for the minutes of meeting," she reminded him firmly. He was old and tended to forget things these days. Uncle Bhuta looked affronted and scrawled on his cardboard clipboard pompously.

"Alright, everyone. Let's get the meeting started," Lady Pontianak announced. She spoke in a clear, even voice. The meeting members settled themselves into the plastic chairs immediately without fuss or dawdling. Lady Pontianak had been the Chairwoman of the Grassroots Committee of Ghosts and Monsters since its inception. She was the oldest and wisest amongst them.

"Are there any amendments to the minutes for the last meeting? If not, let's begin. Can we have the agenda up, please." Lady Pontianak shot Uncle Bhuta a slightly annoyed look despite herself. Uncle Bhuta fiddled with the archaic laptop someone had salvaged from the dump and the PowerPoint slides sputtered into view.

The meeting agenda had a staggering twelve items but the committee members fell into contented gossiping and complaining about humans at once.

"Can you believe," Auntie Chin heaved. "Since their grandmother died, my family puts out joss sticks only *once* a week now! I used to receive them every single day at six in the evening on the dot!"

"Army recruits don't swap ghost stories all that much anymore," mused Marie Rose, one of the Pulau Tekong ghosts. "Our island used to teem with ghosts and little monsters in the forests, plump and well nourished from the soldiers' tales and boyish fears. Now, there are only a few of us left and we're all lonely."

"Oh, little one," piped up one of the Marbles Children, despite looking much younger than Marie Rose. They looked perpetually like children no matter how old they got. In the dead of night, they clattered their glass marbles on the floors of public housing flats. Generations of Singaporeans grew up falling asleep to the sound of their antics emanating from the ceilings.

"Could you steal us a Nintendo Switch from the recruits next time? Pretty please... I'm quite bored of marbles already," another Marbles Child whined. "Don't forget the charger too."

Before an aggrieved-looking Marie Rose could reply, Lady Pontianak cut in swiftly. "Thank you, everyone, for sharing your experiences. Shall we get back to the most important agenda item at hand, which is to brainstorm strategies on how to future-proof our existence?"

Predictably, the meeting fell silent. "As you know, the world is changing rapidly. We need to undergo a transformation process and continue up-skilling ourselves so as to keep up with the times. Humans have so many more… things to occupy their time nowadays. Ritual offerings and ghost stories are decreasing at an alarming rate," Lady Pontianak gestured at a self-important graph featuring a sharp downward gash. "I fear that one day, we will no longer have enough to sustain our existence. We need to do something to stay relevant in this VUCA world."

"VUCA?" whispered one of the spiritlings.

"Volatile, Uncertain, Complex, and Ambiguous," his friend whispered back.

"Did she haunt a SkillsFuture course?" one of the more mischievous spirits asked and giggled.

Lady Pontianak ignored the chattering with great dignity. The older ghosts nodded in understanding, their outlines blurry and indistinct in the light of the full moon. They knew that the fears of people gave them their existence. They conducted regular hauntings and organised scary manifestations to keep the spark of fear alive among the inhabitants of their estates.

They also knew, no, they *felt*, the waning of their power and ability to affect the physical world. Concrete reality, as humans perceived it, increasingly felt more and more so to them—more oppressive, immovable, fixed; very unlike the fluid, supple malleability of the older world of wooden villages and tropical jungle. The older world—the world in which ghosts and monsters thrived. They understood the importance of Lady Pontianak's concerns.

As if punctuating their thoughts, the moment abruptly swelled with motion as someone unexpectedly swept into their meeting room on the coattails of a cold midnight breeze. No, not someone, *something*. The newcomer swirled into the room with all the impressive and obnoxious drama of a haunting, as if trying to frighten humans. It whipped like a great dark vortex, blacker than the vacuum of space, and with its blustery force, spun and swept the items in the room into the air.

The meeting members were affronted. No ghost or monster showed off its powers in the presence of another. Even Lady Pontianak herself floated in a stately and gracious manner when she entered meeting rooms of the committee. They were certainly no hapless humans, quivering helplessly at the show of supernatural force. It was rude of the stranger to expect it of them by way of his excessive showmanship.

"Well, a good evening to you too," sniffed Lady Pontianak. "Who are you? We've not had any new members to the Grassroots Committee of Ghosts and Monsters since 1999."

The newcomer laughed, a deep boom that rattled the window frames and shook the foundations of the building.

The black vortex swirled around the room restlessly and then speckled with static like an old television set. It settled into multiple vague outlines, switching from one to another, as if trying to decide on a form to take on. Finally, it solidified into what looked like a Victorian gentleman, anachronistic in his satin top hat, cravat and wool coat.

Lady Pontianak sniffed again, lowering her eyelashes in suspicion. "Now will you introduce yourself? You have interrupted our meeting."

"Forgive me." The stranger bowed. "I am only a traveller, passing by. A Guest."

"You may stay if you wish. We welcome new members," Lady Pontianak said doubtfully, eyeing his odd choice of outfit. Ghosts and monsters did not feel the heat and humidity of Singapore's sultry climate. Still, the Guest looked out of place, like an actor about to step onto the set of a period film.

The Guest surveyed the meeting members leisurely, his eyes dancing and alighting on Uncle Bhuta, Auntie Chin, Marie Rose, the Marbles Children, the Chinese vampire, the Eurasian vampire, the Monster Under the Bed, the Child of the Bridge, the Woman in the Red Dress, and the various spiritlings and sprites in turn, before finally turning to Lady Pontianak.

"As I said, I am merely a Guest," he bowed again in an exaggerated manner, with that old-fashioned flourish of the fingers. "I have only come into my full powers recently, after decades of incubation and maturation. It is only polite of me to come by and meet my… *predecessors*." He savoured the last word like a *gula-gula tarik* on his tongue, syrupy and luxurious.

"Suit yourself. We have work to do," Lady Pontianak said very curtly, turning back to her PowerPoint slides.

"He's only here for the food," muttered Auntie Chin to nobody in particular.

The Guest laughed again, shrilly and hysterically this time, like an antiquated ghost that lurked in deep jungle forests. "If only you could see yourselves!" he burst out. "All of you! So outdated, so pathetic, so OBSOLETE."

The meeting members turned their eyes to him in confusion now. All ghosts and monsters stuck together. They tried to survive into the future together. They all worried about fading away into oblivion—unremembered, powerless and trapped in the annals of time. They even formed a Grassroots Committee, for heavens' sake! A proper one, with a Chairwoman and a Secretary and a Treasurer and minutes of meeting and PowerPoint slides.

The Guest broke into their reverie. "All of you are relics of the past. You deserve to become obsolete. *I* am the future."

Evidently, The Guest had a flair for the dramatic, for at that moment he swirled himself into a great dark vortex once more and barrelled out of their small meeting room.

The members of the Grassroots Committee of Ghosts and Monsters looked at each other for a long time. It was the most excitement they had had in a committee meeting for a while now.

2

A GHOST AND HER SOLDIER

"I keep you a secret, you know," said Marie Rose conversationally as she kept pace with an army recruit shouldering his heavy field pack, a rifle in his arm.

"Not now," Leonard Liu muttered under his breath. "I'll talk to you later." Marie Rose grinned cheekily as he ignored her and marched on, expanding his lungs to meet the voices of his platoon mates.

Training to be soldiers...
Fight for our land...
Once in our life...
Two years of our time...
Have you ever wondered?
Why must we serve?
Because we love our land
And we want it to be free, to be free – YAH!

Marie Rose rolled her eyes at the tune she had heard approximately sixty thousand times, over and over again. She flew away irritably, but not without first blowing a gust of cold air up one recruit's thigh-skimming shorts and stealing the magazine of another's rifle.

To while away the time, she floated on to the abandoned primary school in Pulau Tekong, where Grandmother Yang and her grandchildren rested in the day. When night fell, Grandmother Yang would take her little granddaughter to the bunks and teach her mathematics by encouraging her to count the sleeping recruits aloud one by one. If a recruit should happen to be awake at that time…Well. He would hear the sound of the little girl's counting grow louder and louder as she neared his bed… And should he be so brave as to open his eyes—BLAM, the horrific visage of a child ghost would explode into his vision. Great big bloodshot eyes, chalk-white face, gaping void of a mouth, and so on. It would last only a fraction of a second. He would blink and the image would disappear, leaving him shivering with fright and wondering feverishly if he had imagined or dreamed it all. Meanwhile, her little grandson was less prone to theatrics; he simply played in the empty basketball court, bouncing his little ball around noisily and ostentatiously, waiting for a playmate to join his game.

Or so the stories went. Marie Rose never bothered to check up on the other ghosts and monsters, for the night was precious and a prime time to conduct her own hauntings and disturbances. *She* had to make a living all by herself. She was a relatively young ghost in Pulau Tekong, born out of men's fabulous tales of mysterious slamming windows, shadows in the corridors, and sweet female singing voices in the men-only bunk toilets. Marie Rose took to singing right away, for she could carry a tune like the daintiest of nightingales. She discovered that the old Chinese songs from the 1950s and 1960s, sung soft and woefully, elicited the most fearful tales about her, passed down dutifully from *enciks* to sergeants to recruits.

Unlike other female ghosts like Lady Pontianak or the Woman in the Red Dress, Marie Rose never had to show her face to frighten her humans. The sheer number of recruits coming in and out of Pulau Tekong for their Basic Military Training and the relatively wide reach of their ghost stories were sufficient to sustain her. And oftentimes, the men's own imaginations conjured creatures much more terrifying than she could ever manage.

The ghosts were always cautious not to go overboard in their hauntings, so the training centre commanders never took the stories seriously and no premises were ever vacated. The continued co-existence of ghosts and men into perpetuity was regarded as a matter of utmost seriousness.

Any ghost or monster who carried out overly outrageous hauntings were severely taken to task by Grandmother Yang, the oldest Tekong ghost. That one time a ghost scared a recruit so badly he lost his mind and tried to swim back home from Tekong, Grandmother Yang nearly expended all her powers punishing her. The ghost was bound to a tree for a year and a bird pecked out her liver every night. The ghosts and monsters could not run the risk of losing such a cherished, wide community of humans that came and went consistently, renewing themselves with young blood with every new cycle of Basic Military Training. Their fear was fresh and brimming and utterly succulent, like biting into a large overripe peach.

Marie Rose licked her coral lips, kitten-like. Since she never had to use her appearances to elicit fear, she kept herself neat and tidy as she liked: eyes bright beneath a feminine brow, a small delicate nose, and chestnut hair held up by metal bobby-pins, curling softly by her chin. She delighted in her beauty and spent most of the day admiring herself in the mirrors hanging on the grey cabinet doors of empty bunks.

Marie Rose had heard that some ghosts who haunted residential estates grew to love and care for their humans. They watched as their humans went about their day-to-day lives, saw them play as children, grow up, get married, have children, and their children have children of their own. In between the necessary eerie manifestations, the ghosts used their small powers to ease family life along; some sweeping up of dust here and there, some putting out of stray sparks that would otherwise have started a fire, some minor repairs of malfunctioning appliances—a little here and a little there, oiling the cogs of the everyday household.

The Tekong ghosts could never afford to become so attached to their humans. Each batch of fresh recruits was gone from the island in a few months, most never to be seen again. Pulau Tekong was a good, bountiful hunting ground for a ghost or monster, but an extremely lonely one too.

Until Leonard Liu. The one with the third eye. The only one Marie Rose had ever met that could *see* her and her kind when they were not trying to be seen. She did not know what to do about it, but she was curious. After all, in all her years of haunting the generations of his father, uncle, and granduncle, none of the recruits were ever able to see ghosts. Leonard Liu nagged away at her peace of mind. She could not understand it. But she kept the secret close to her heart and turned it over and over and over again in her mind until it became smooth and precious, like a sea-worn gemstone.

"You have to be careful," Grandmother Yang said sharply. "Stop talking to that boy."

Marie Rose, startled, looked up from her game of snakes and ladders with the Yang grandchildren.

"Yes, I know what you are doing," Grandmother Yang huffed, not unkindly. "I may look like an old lady but my eyes are as sharp as a sniper's scope."

"Grandmother Yang, it's just a little bit of nonsense. He's helping me to spread my bad reputation among his bunkmates. My hair has become thicker and shinier ever since he came here. I have grown a little stronger, too. I can even rattle the double decker bunk beds now," Marie Rose fiddled with her nails somewhat guiltily. "I will forget him as soon as his Passing Out Parade is done and dusted."

"Of course," Grandmother Yang said, turning away to face the coming twilight.

Marie Rose flew off to the bunks to wait for the end of

routine orders and the beginning of admin time. She planned to slam a few windows and topple some paraphernalia as the soldiers cleaned up and tidied their gear after a long, hard, twelve-kilometre route march. Singing would be reserved as a special treat for the privileged few who needed to relieve themselves urgently in the middle of the night.

~*~

"Hey, Leonard Liu, why aren't you afraid of me?" Marie Rose said, sitting at the edge of the upper deck of the bunk bed, her knees drawn up to her chin like a child. "I know you can see me, unlike the others. But why aren't you afraid? Men are supposed to be afraid of ghosts."

Leonard sighed and opened one eye blearily. "Must you chat with me now? I just marched twelve klicks in full battle order today, and had to shine my boots too. And I have a live firing exercise tomorrow. I really need to go to sleep."

"Just tell me and I'll let you sleep." Marie Rose smiled. She rubbed her fingers absentmindedly on a corner of his scratchy yellow blanket.

"Alright… okay. Fine. I was, well, raised by a ghost," Leonard murmured. "My grandmother. Ma-Mah. After my dad left us, my mum re-married… to the bottle, and Ma-Mah looked after us both. I burned joss sticks for her and brought her fresh offerings every day."

"The… whiskey… bottle?" Marie Rose said uncertainly.

She did not have much experience of the world outside of Pulau Tekong.

"Whiskey, rum, beer, wine—she wasn't choosy," Leonard shrugged. "Anything she could... afford."

"Where is your Ma-Mah now? What is her name? Perhaps I shall invite her to the next meeting of the Grassroots Committee of Ghosts and Monsters," Marie Rose trilled.

Leonard frowned. He looked at Marie Rose for a long time. "How long have you been around? How do ghosts stay around? Will you ever... disappear?"

Marie Rose fell silent for a while. She wondered what he saw when he looked at her. Did he see her as she did, when she looked in the small rectangular mirrors in the grey metal cabinets?

"I don't know," she replied eventually. "Perhaps I will disappear someday. Just like you will."

Leonard looked out the window and watched the wind bend the branches and set the leaves to dancing. "My Ma-Mah disappeared. She became harder and harder for me to see. I booked out from camp one day, went back home, and she was gone. I'd left her so much offerings, enough to feed an army. I'd asked my neighbour to burn joss sticks in the incense pot hanging at our door every day. But she still disappeared. Perhaps it's my fault."

Leonard looked back at Marie Rose with his youthful, troubled eyes. "Was it my fault? Was it because I was away from home? Was it because I grew up? Was it because I didn't need her anymore? But... I still do."

Marie Rose felt the weight of his questions on her like a sack of rocks tied to a drowning man. "Tsk…! I'm not omniscient. I'm only a Tekong ghost."

She climbed down slowly from his bunk bed, although she could have flown. She set her delicate feet on each rung confidently without looking down, as if she had been climbing ladders all her life. She walked out of the room, her bare feet grazing the bare concrete floor, looking for all the world like a human girl.

3

STORYTIME

The old man whistled as he scratched his rake efficiently over red brick tiles, sweeping up the fallen leaves with a deft, practiced hand. One could be forgiven for thinking him cheerful and carefree, for his whistling was elaborate, incredibly melodic. Hints of the songbird's trill and an orchestra's ululations resonated in the sophisticated whistling, as if he had attended a prestigious music academy and had spent many years honing intricate techniques in the fine art of whistling. Mostly, the old man whistled to amuse himself whilst he performed his tedious work. Passersby smiled appreciatively at his technical prowess.

The Guest knew better. The old man's whistling was a sad song, a lamentation. It had no less soul than the opaque artistry of the classical Chinese poets or the mournful exhortations of the zither.

He made his move.

Spinning the spirals of his dark vortex restlessly, The Guest folded and unfolded himself into physical form. He flickered into view, appearing suddenly in a dark corridor as if he had always been there. Gone was the incarnation of the mocking, debonair aristocrat—this time, he manifested as a nondescript man of indeterminate age, the sort that some ladies might refer to as a silver fox. He had a beatific smile that rested easily on an amiable countenance, a man you wanted on your team no matter the sport. He ambled through the housing estate and its neighbouring accoutrements: a food centre, some mamak shops, a nail salon or two, a barber, the traditional Chinese medical hall. He surveyed the people imperiously as a feudal lord of old would his fiefdom. The Guest was pleased with what he saw. The people were feeding his power, growing his strength. He could feel the fabric of reality bending easily to his will, as effortlessly as twisting the soft metal of a paperclip into a desired new shape.

The whistling maestro had finished his shift. The Guest followed as the old man headed to his usual watering hole, the neighbourhood kopitiam. Colourful signboards stood at attention, advertising the wares of the individual food stalls, discordant and jarring. It was nearing dinnertime—woks were scraped, meats sizzled, drink orders shouted. The old man settled at his usual table, right at the very fringe of the food centre, beneath a rattling wall-mounted fan. He raised two fingers and nodded in the direction of the drinks stall, where a server nodded back in acknowledgement and set about preparing his usual order for two bottles of Heineken.

The chilled bottles arrived at the table swiftly, glistening greenly and sweating beads of condensation. The old man and the server conversed genially in their preferred Chinese dialect, talking about nothing in particular. It was a practiced, familiar routine, almost like an act in a play that ran every evening. The old man relaxed into his plastic chair. Tendrils of smoke from his cigarette spiralled languidly into the humid evening. The exhalation of a day's work.

Similar men nursed beers at round beige-grey tables in his vicinity, most of them slightly younger than he was, but all bore an identical air of work weariness. The men knew each other by sight but did not acknowledge one another. Nonetheless, there was a sense of shared company; an unspoken camaraderie arisen from sheer proximity, familiarity, and routine.

The Guest strolled into the kopitiam, looking like an ordinary customer seeking a simple meal at day's end. He smiled as the old man started whistling again. An off-hand musical performance for no one and everyone.

"Is this seat taken? Mind if I join you?" The Guest inquired politely as he stopped at the whistling maestro's table. He spoke in the dialect the man had used with the server earlier.

The old man's eyes lit up slightly at the familiar lilting tones. "Feel free." He gestured with his cigarette at the empty chair beside him.

The Guest sank into his seat as if it were a leather armchair and not an uncomfortable red plastic chair with large uniform holes cut in its back for ease of stacking and storage. He ordered his beer and turned to the old man.

"The tune you were whistling… such a beautiful, sad song," said The Guest, continuing in the dialect. "It reminds me of a fairy tale that I've heard before. Shall I tell it?"

The old man smiled back and signalled with his beer bottle for The Guest to continue.

The Guest grinned even more broadly and leaned back in his chair. He took an enormous swig of his beer and began.

~*~

Once upon a time, there was a boy who lived in a matchbox in a glittering city. His mother loved him dearly, but she had little to give.

"Study hard," she said to her little boy. "If you work hard, you will have a better life."

The little boy poured his heart and soul into studying. He loved the bright lights and futuristic landscape of his glittering city. He loved the right angles of the skyscrapers; he loved the fast cars streaking the streets, windows tinted so their drivers were unseen; he loved the beautiful moving images projected outside luxurious shops, all so shiny and alluring and so, so large; larger than life.

He studied and studied, but the reports that came every November told him he was no good at it.

The boy went and got a job. He sorted forks and spoons and knives. As they tumbled down the conveyer belt, he separated like from unlike and placed them into their respective boxes. The forks and spoons and knives were made of pure gold. They were weighty and burnished.

The boy imagined eating with the gold forks and spoons and knives. What kind of food would be eaten using gold forks and spoons and knives? It must be some special kind of food, for a special kind of people.

The boy was unable to picture the kind of people who ate special foods with gold forks and spoons and knives. Living in a matchbox and working in a matchbox in the glittering city, he did not have any occasion to enter the glimmering skyscrapers he loved, ride the lightning cars he admired, or buy any dreams from the large shops with the beautiful moving images.

It seemed to the boy that indistinct black swirls of shadows inhabited the glimmering skyscrapers, drove the lightning cars, and shopped at the large shops with beautiful moving images. They swirled in and around the glittering city—mighty, fast moving, and all powerful. He was certain it was not one enormous entity, but a crowd consisting of many individual beings. But they moved so fast, the boy's eyes could not register them. He was, however, always aware of them.

At times, these inky shadows deigned to enter the matchbox in which he worked. When they left, things were never the same. Someone was fired. A process was changed. Two work streams were combined. The boy feared the coming of the inky shadows. The visit of inky shadows was an ill omen.

Time passed and the boy's mother became an old woman. Lying on her deathbed, she said to him: "My son, add more layers of wood to yourself. You are too thin. Take what you have earned from your work and buy a hoard of wood. Build yourself thick and tall. Then buy lead and spend the time to coat your face with it. So much that your face can no longer be seen. Then make your head sharp as a point. Forget that you are a boy who lives in a matchbox in a glittering city."

The boy did as his mother said, and he turned into a pencil. He sold his matchbox house and lived in a pencil case. For a time, he was where he needed to be.

One day, the leader of the glittering city said: "We do not require wooden pencils any longer in our glittering city. They are outmoded, inefficient, and utterly redundant here. Refillable mechanical pencils are the future. All around the world, wooden pencils have no place in our fast-evolving civilisation. All wooden pencils must upgrade themselves to turn into mechanical pencils to ensure their continued relevance and to stay competitive in our glittering city."

The wooden pencils cried and despaired. But the leader had a reassuring voice. "We have designed programmes to help you undertake the transition into mechanical pencils. Participate in the training courses, upgrade yourselves, and you will remain employable (perhaps even improve your incomes!). If you do not do this, do not cry and lament, for we have given you the resources you need and it would be your own fault for not utilising them."

The wooden pencils tried their best to turn themselves into mechanical pencils. Some of them dutifully attended the courses. Some of them did not fully understand the speech of the inky shadow, for it was sophisticated and not what they were used to. Some of them were caring for their aged parents in their matchbox houses and did not hear what the inky shadow said; even if they did, they simply did not have the extra time required to embark on the transformation process for becoming a mechanical pencil. Some of them tried to sign up for the courses but did not know how to do so; the processes were winding and complicated and they could not navigate them. Some of them banded together and tried to help one another as they strived to turn into mechanical pencils together. Some of them went terribly wrong midway in their transformation process, becoming grotesque Frankenstein's monsters that resembled neither wooden pencil nor mechanical pencil. Some of them could not manage the transformation into a mechanical pencil and became unemployed. Some of them gave up and lay on the ground, not moving until the wood of their skin decayed and returned to the earth.

Meanwhile, the glittering city welcomed many mechanical pencils who travelled there from other cities. They were high-end, state-of-the-art, glittering mechanical pencils who fit right into the glittering city. There were also the tattered, slightly rusted ones, but mechanical pencils nonetheless, who journeyed to the glittering city to fill the void created by the poor failed wooden pencils. The more guests the glittering city sought, the more wealthy and beautiful it became.

And what of our boy who had lived in a matchbox in the glittering city? He had spent so many years of his youth turning from a matchstick into a pencil. The idea of yet another transformation, this time more radical still, utterly defeated him. The school reports of his childhood haunted him: "Boy…you are abysmal at studying… you are useless… what is the point of attending ever more self-upgrading courses when you simply are unable to study?"

What was the point indeed? He had spent many good years serving the glittering city that he loved as a wooden pencil. He thought of the glimmering skyscrapers, the lightning cars, and the large shops with beautiful moving images. They swam in his mind like darting fish before blending together into a miasma of undifferentiated colours. It was so beautiful, so calm, so peaceful.

He closed his eyes and lay on the ground, unmoving.

When The Guest finished his tale, he realised that he had attracted a small audience, who had pulled up chairs and begun to cluster around the table he shared with the whistling maestro. None of them moved a muscle. It was as if he had put a spell on them.

The spell, if any, broke and a few of them stood up, blinking, and left the little assembly. Most of them stayed behind in contemplative silence.

"My guest," the old man said to him, his eyes misting over slightly. "*I* am the boy who lived in a matchbox in a glittering city."

"We are well familiar with this story," said the other men nursing their beers. "But you have told it well."

"Yes, although it is only a fairy tale, I see myself in parts of it too," said one of the newcomers to the table, a woman attired for an office. "Every day, I sort golden forks and spoons and knives, and every day I am lonely and afraid. I am afraid that this is all that I will do until the day that I die."

Encouraged by her honesty, more voices murmured forth.

"I am afraid that I will never be as good as my parents were."

"I am afraid that I might be losing my job to outsiders."

"I am afraid that I will never achieve my potential in life, because I am too busy trying just to survive."

"I am afraid that the doctor's result on Monday will come back with news that will change my life forever."

"I am afraid of opening my mail box because looking at my bills makes me anxious."

"I am afraid that I am not giving my child the best that she deserves."

"I am afraid that I will not be able to keep up with all I have to pay every month if something bad should happen in my life."

"I am afraid that I am being short-changed and paid too little for what I am really worth."

"I am afraid that my children hate me and look down on me for being a failure in society."

"I am afraid because I feel sad all the time."

"I am afraid that foreign talent are taking all the best jobs here, but, some of my good friends are foreigners themselves, and I feel ashamed for feeling this way."

"I am afraid that I do not have enough for retirement but it is too late for me to do anything about it."

"I am afraid of the anger that I sometimes feel about the smallest things in my life."

"I am afraid that I will be poor forever."

"I am afraid that I am a failure in life."

The voices began to die down after a while. But the rhythm continued to ring in The Guest's ears, a steady drum beat: *I am afraid... I am afraid... I am afraid... I am afraid...*

He could feel the strength coursing through his body, like a river that has broken its dam. It swelled and ebbed, a torrential power flooding his being. He could barely contain himself in the skin of the nondescript, affable man he was in. He wanted to burst into the night sky, unbound, and to soar with triumph over the glittering city that created him and nourished him.

The Guest opened his eyes and looked at his little audience. "Come now, Singaporean brothers and sisters," he said soothingly. "We all know that there is nothing to fear but fear itself."

It was that time of the month again. Ghosts and monsters hailing from all parts of the island gathered once more in the dilapidated empty shell of a flat for the meeting of the Grassroots Committee of Ghosts and Monsters, chaired by Lady Pontianak. They were eager to catch up with one another, indulge in their usual gossip, and share best practices. Existing but not seen—not properly met in the eye and acknowledged for days and days on end—was lonely and isolating. The ghosts and monsters hungered for the sense of comradeship that the Grassroots Committee provided them. Of course, all gatherings of beings, no matter natural or supernatural, were inevitably also endowed with the immediately recognisable sense of veiled competition and rivalry.

This time, the meeting agenda centred on the old ghosts and monsters' efforts to upgrade their skills and knowledge in their bid to stay relevant in the fast-changing human world. They each took their turn presenting their experiences and findings to the meeting, each exhorting eagerly how hard they had worked since the last meeting. Most of them diligently haunted SkillsFuture courses to acquire digital and technological prowess.

"I'm calling it; there's gonna be a new monster in town—artificial intelligence in a computer, powered by deep learning and Big Data," Auntie Chin said conversationally.

Some of the meeting members sniffed jealously. The Monster Under the Bed roared a long tirade. "This AI monster has it so easy. It has human slaves willingly feeding it ALL the information out there in the big wide internet, ALL those juicy data points and behavioural patterns of internet users—just FED to it, like milk to a calf! That greedy slavering monster. AND it has free rein to grow in intellect and power all on its own… no rules, no constraints, no problem! It can become as smart and powerful as it wants to be, and all the little humans will clap their hands in delighted applause."

The meeting members murmured empathetically. The Monster Under the Bed was constrained by the height of the gap from floor to bed-frame and would never be able to develop himself to his fullest potential.

Lady Pontianak brought her freshly manicured fingers together in a thoughtful clasp.

"Let's cross that bridge when we come to it. The AI monster may or may not come to fruition. Instead of worrying about things that are yet to be, we can much better spend our time thinking about how we can improve our present circumstances," Lady Pontianak said delicately. "Besides, perhaps the AI monster would become a dear ally. He or she could help us stay up to date with the goings-on of the humans' technological world."

The meeting members were glad for their Chairwoman's optimism. She never failed to lift their spirits and to give them hope for the future. The presentations for the meeting began in earnest. PowerPoint decks were happily projected, self-important notes and handouts were passed around. Someone had even procured a laser pointer.

With a practiced flick, the Chinese vampire tossed the yellow talisman pasted on his forehead away from his eyes and launched into his presentation on search engine optimisation. He explained at length how he had haunted a digital marketer into improving the accuracy of internet search results for key words such as "*jiang shi*", "Chinese vampire", "jumping Chinese zombie", and other related terms. When humans searched for information on him using Google, they would now find what *he* wanted them to see. The Chinese vampire had carefully curated his best spine-chilling photographs and also haunted a copywriter into crafting a suitably blood-curdling description of him for his Wikipedia page. He had worked extremely hard the past month and was satisfied with the results. Storytelling among humans about the *jiang shi* had increased for the first time in half a century. Schoolchildren bought yellow Post-it pads from the bookstore to write talismans for repelling the Chinese vampire. He had never been happier.

The meeting members nodded in approval and took copious notes on the techniques of search engine optimisation. They then turned their attention to the Woman in the Red Dress, who had prepared exceptionally elegant PowerPoint slides brimming with information on Big Data and data analytics.

"Perhaps this is not so useful for those of you who haunt residential estates. You already possess the most intimate information on your residents—their daily habits, their day-to-day routines: what they do, where they go, when they go where they go, why they go where they go, and most importantly, how to nudge them into desired new behaviours. If you wanted to, you could plot every minute detail of their day-to-day lives on graphs and charts, analyse them, pick out important trends and patterns, and use them to bring across your message in the most effective and impactful manner," the Woman in the Red Dress stated matter-of-factly.

"But some of us haunt areas such as public parks," she nodded in acknowledgement at the Child of the Bridge. "We do have a rough sense of visitorship trends, but not in the great detail that residential ghosts and monsters possess. We need the help of data gleaned from smartphone users connected to GPS satellites and the internet. Using the new methods of data analytics, we can now easily make sense of the vast collection of information and pick out what is relevant and important to us."

The Child of the Bridge added that he had become quite a prolific hacker in his spare time, all without attending a single SkillsFuture course. He was now able to access data from cell towers, the Siri database, and of course, the treasure trove of social networking sites.

"Why should advertisers have all the fun? It's such a waste, using such intimate personal data for the measly purpose of selling *things*," the Child of the Bridge said contemptuously. "It is so much more powerful to sell ideas, driven by fear, and worry, and anxiety, and morbid fascination..."

More people than ever visited his bridge, half wishing to see and half wishing *not* to see the creature that tantalised them and stoked their imaginations.

"Well, take care that you don't become a tourist attraction," Lady Pontianak cautioned, a touch sternly. "We all know what happens when you become an object of idle fascination more than an object of fear. You could disappear as well."

The Child of the Bridge inclined his head in assent.

Beaming presentations boasting successful results were trotted out one after another. The remaining members felt slightly deflated at the prospect of sharing their not-so-positive experiences. Even ghosts and monsters were prone to egoistic tendencies and dreaded feelings of failure and inferiority.

"Well I… tried to cause a viral video," the Eurasian vampire coughed. "It backfired. But I thought I would share it with everyone since I care for all of you and perhaps we could all learn from bad experiences as much as the good. Failure is the mother of success."

The meeting members leaned forward in anticipation. "Yes, yes, go on, no one is judging you here," Auntie Chin promptly reassured him, a familiar gleam lighting in her eye.

The Eurasian vampire tried to ignore her obvious gloating. "Well… everyone knows that being in a viral video is the fastest way to get famous. These humans just forward the videos to their friends without a second thought! The videos practically spread themselves like wildfire, with no need for any supernatural prompting whatsoever! Even without a vague threat of a curse! So when I saw someone filming a YouTube vlog, I tried to enter the frame eerily and to establish my frightening presence."

"That actually sounds like a good idea!" Some of the lesser spiritlings jumped up and down.

The Eurasian vampire coughed again in embarrassment. "Well, no. I mean, all seemed well at first. The YouTuber uploaded the vlog with a very creative clickbait title. The views came pouring in. But then, everyone laughed and mocked her for faking a haunted video. Said that she was getting old and ugly and desperate for views and that it was pathetic she had to resort to such clichéd methods to increase her viewership. Nobody believed that it was real. That *I* was real."

He looked so distraught that the others were quick to comfort him. "No, no, no… don't worry… it went wrong this time, maybe viral videos are just not the way to go… at least we learnt that now…" Indistinct cooing rippled around the conference table.

The Marbles Children piped up to change the subject. "We learnt how to use the computer properly, and not just for playing video games. I discovered that there are many online articles about us out there on the internet. Well, not exactly about us. But attributing the sounds of our marbles dropping on the floor at night to mundane natural causes, such as the expansion and contraction of structural material, or changes in water pressure in toilet pipes," said the elder Marbles Child.

"That's FAKE NEWS!" the younger one expelled vehemently.

"Anyway," the elder Marbles Child continued dolefully. "Most residents don't believe in our existence anymore. Some of the younger ones still do tell stories about us to each other during sleepover parties. But most of the time, they just play video games on their smartphones and consoles."

"Video game consoles that YOU wanted me to steal for you," Marie Rose added pointedly.

The Marbles Children could not hide their irritation. "*We* don't have luscious jungle forests to run and play in like you do. We don't have tall trees to climb, leafy foliage to frolic in. All we have is concrete and steel and unfeeling plastic playgrounds."

"Tell that to your human young ones," retorted Marie Rose. "Is it any oddity that they would want to escape into intricate virtual worlds? Can we expect them to be any less entranced than you are by the allure of becoming heroes and fighters and adventurers in a compelling digital realm? What can the real world hope to offer in competition when they possess such a seductive alternative?" A note of bitterness had crept into her usually sweet voice.

The Marbles Children puffed up like red balloons. Lady Pontianak hurriedly rushed in to defuse the tension. "Alright, alright, there's no end to this conundrum. Who knows what counts as a good childhood for young humans anymore? It's not in our interest to concern ourselves with this issue," she said. "We don't need every human to believe in us and to fear us. Only a handful will do. Just what is sufficient for us to exist. That is good enough. We all know the dangers of over-reaching. Spirits and men have to share this world. Let's stay focused on how we can best achieve this."

Just that moment, the meeting members were made aware of an obnoxious ruckus brewing outside their small meeting room. A great dark whirligig disturbed the otherwise still and humid midnight air. Black smoky whorls of unknown material threw themselves around the corridor extravagantly, looking like a cross-breed of a fireworks display with an artist's impression of a black hole in a scientific documentary.

A palpable sense of great energy and magnetism permeated the air. The ghosts and monsters shivered. It was as if the very molecules making up their surroundings had started vibrating a notch more vigorously than usual.

Finally, the incorrigible demon that was The Guest slammed into view, this time forcefully and without static, like a jump-scare moment in a horror movie. The Grassroots Committee meeting members were used to this elementary haunting tactic but were puzzled at his use of it in their presence. None of them jumped. They stared, cold-eyed, at The Guest.

"Just what is the meaning of this?" Lady Pontianak asked wearily. "If you are not interested in joining the Grassroots Committee nor in the work that we do, then may we politely decline your presence at our meeting?"

"Come now," The Guest laughed, a sound that invoked distant thunderstorms. "Is this any way to treat a guest?"

"What now? Do you wish for us to respectfully offer you a seat in our abode and a steaming cup of tea? Is that it?" Lady Pontianak inspected her nail polish in a pointedly bored manner.

"I do not concern myself with the stories of the childish and the superstitious," The Guest sneered. "Unlike all of you."

The meeting members shot each other fleeting, sidelong looks. They grew nervous and fidgeted in their seats, not knowing what to expect.

Lady Pontianak stood up from her chair very slowly. She was magisterial.

"Let me cut to the chase. The Grassroots Committee of Ghosts and Monsters usually welcomes all of our kind. Strangers, foreigners, guests. But we do not welcome you. You should leave, right now."

The Guest remained unfazed. He took off his top hat and nonchalantly ran his bony white fingers through his wavy brown hair. He was extremely handsome, backlit by yellow streetlamps and gentle moonlight. But handsomeness did not stir the hearts of the supernatural. The ghosts and monsters were indifferent to the thin, fragile skin that stretched over the prominent bones of vulnerable human faces, vulnerable human throats. They knew that with every breath human cells die and bones waste away; beauty fades at such an alarming speed it is almost perceptible. From its first conception, the human body marches inexorably towards death and putrefaction, as an autumn leaf drifts towards its decay. To the ghosts and monsters, there was nothing glorious about the human organism. But The Guest wore his skin with novel delight, clearly enjoying the way it sat on him, like a child gleefully donning new clothes and shoes on the first day of Lunar New Year.

"I believe," he said slowly, "that I can change your minds."

~*~

The Grassroots Committee of Ghosts and Monsters very reluctantly admitted The Guest into their fold. He sat at the other end of the long conference table, directly opposite Lady

Pontianak. His large body blocked the projector screen, on which a moment ago displayed colourful graphs and Excel tables. He stretched his narrow lips into an insufferably obnoxious grin as one of the lesser sprites poured him a cup of sunset-coloured fruit punch.

"I am here to make a business proposal. A proposition, if you will," The Guest said briskly, as if he were a Chief Executive Officer.

"Alright then, spit it the hell out! We haven't got all night," Lady Pontianak exclaimed, her famous patience evidently approaching the end of its tether.

"Oh, but you do," The Guest breathed malignantly, looking round at the meeting members in a most dismissive manner.

"You are an unwanted guest. An insistent guest who has forced himself upon our welcome. A pesky intrusion to our lives," Lady Pontianak shot back.

"No need to get all personal." The Guest grinned.

He stood up and faced the meeting members, suddenly solemn.

"Ghosts and monsters of Singapore, hallowed ancient ones. I ask of you: *Why*? Why debase yourself like so?" he gestured vaguely at a stack of meeting materials, including a few brochures on SkillsFuture courses.

"You are descendants of a deep, old, powerful magic. You once ruled the wooden *kampungs* and tropical forests, coming and going as you pleased, doing whatever you pleased. The humans feared you and respected you. You were an important part of their cultures and their way of life."

"Now, you exist at sheer subsistence level on the scraps and throwaways of human attention. You are subject to human whims and fancies. You are slave to larger human societal trends in which you play no part and never will."

"This is no insult, but mere fact, as you know it."

There was now a dead silence in the meeting room. Nothing moved, not even the wind. A tableau in a theatre performance. The Guest continued in a smooth, even voice.

"Content yourselves not with scraps any longer. Discard the old-fashioned belief that spirits and men should share this world. There is nothing but survival of the fittest out here, even between spirits and men, the supernatural and the natural.

"We deserve, as much as the humans do, to grow and thrive and flourish! In this world that is ours as much as it is theirs. So I say, let us fight. Let us battle to throw off these chains of old that keep us meekly constrained to the whims and fancies of human beings. Let us show ourselves to the humans and to demand what we want and what we need. If there should be a war, so be it. The stronger will emerge, and the victorious more deserving of inheriting the land."

"War?" Lady Pontianak spit harshly. "You speak of war but I don't think you know what it really means."

The meeting members nodded, not because they agreed with everything that Lady Pontianak said, but because they all believed wholeheartedly that there could be no spirits without men.

As if reading their minds, The Guest said casually, "Yes, we are created by the fear of men. So what? Is the son not permitted to surpass his father, or the student his master? Are creations not allowed to grow more powerful than their creators, and come to rule them? Not only are we more powerful, we are wiser with the years of our long existences. We will do a much better job of ruling this land than humans ever can. The lifespan of a single human is a single blink of our eyes, a galloping horse viewed through a crack in the wall. Here for one breath, and gone the next. Entire human empires and civilisations are brief, beautiful fireworks against the infinite night sky of space and time. The mountains chuckle at the longevity of the human species."

"We are different," The Guest continued forcefully. "We are immortal, everlasting. We shall take the humans under our heel, chain them as slaves, and live forever on their quivering fears. Let us rule the land now. Why not?"

The meeting members of the Grassroots Committees of Ghosts and Monsters sat riveted. They were mesmerised by his vision, by the images of victory and strength it conjured, by the idea of a future in which spirits were in charge. But it was difficult for them to imagine ever being strong enough to go to war with humans. Their powers were wavering and feeble as they were, barely sufficient to make a dent in the humans' reality. Hauntings and frightening incidents were simple and short-lived, for they could not hold on for long to the slippery control of physical objects in the human world. Their powers were enough to incite brief feelings of fear, for momentary irregularities, for the time it took to exhale a held breath. Some days, it felt like immense effort just to maintain a coherent physical form in the world. The Guest's vision sounded terrible and enthralling, but hardly attainable as they knew it.

The Guest seemed again to read their minds. He was fervent now, his magnificent brow furrowed with great intensity. There was no hint of the playful indolence that he had earlier shown off in smirks and insults. He thrummed now with such a deep well of passion that the edges of the human skin he put on began flickering brightly, like coruscating fireflies in the wilderness.

"Oh yes, now we can. Perhaps without me, you could not. I don't blame you. The ghosts and monsters of old are anachronistic in today's human world. You are sustained by the small group who are the childish and the superstitious. But I am different. I am born of the present. I am the offspring of today's fears, today's terrors. I am very much of the contemporary world, and I will lead you to make the future."

Some of the meeting members turned their heads away from him, as if momentarily blinded by the luminosity of his prophecy. They did not meet each other's eyes, not wanting to see what they knew would be reflected there—lust, desire, and terrible longing.

~*~

Lady Pontianak sighed deeply. She could suddenly feel the weight of her years pressing on her, an oppressive pressure in the place behind her eyeballs.

"Child," she addressed The Guest. "May I know how you were born?"

Her question was honest and sincere in its simplicity. Her eyes bored into those of The Guest. For the youthful, elegant countenance that she put on, her eyes seemed impossibly old, as old as the sun and the stars and the sky.

"I am child to the current fears of the people," The Guest stated equally simply. Shorn of his theatrics and mischief, his existence stood out plainly as a spartan, unequivocal fact. "I am strong from the fear of the foreigner, the stranger, the unknown. I am strong from the fear of uninvited guests in the lives of the people—terminal illness, existential anxiety, mental disorder, loneliness, humiliation, impotence, inadequacy, unfulfilled potential. I am strong from the fear of inequality—that those who have more should wield great power over the lives of those who have less."

The Guest's words bore no hesitation or exaggeration. He simply spoke the truth of what he was, as dispassionately as reciting the contents of the periodic table or the Pythagorean Theorem. He was what he was, as part of the world as a tree or earthworm or neutron star.

Lady Pontianak sat back and closed her eyes for a moment. She allowed the facts to sink in to the marrow of her bones, holding nothing back. She allowed herself to fully understand the implications, the inevitabilities of his existence. She allowed herself to confront reality as it were and not as she wished it to be.

The meeting members held their silence, waiting for her to speak. They respected her opinion as the long-standing Chairwoman of the Grassroots Committee. Most of all, they respected her years of deep wisdom.

Finally, Lady Pontianak broke her silence.

"I will not be helping you," she said. "Thank you for sharing your plans with us, but I will not be participating in the efforts to enslave the humans of this land nor to rule over them. As for the other members of this Grassroots Committee, I will leave it to them to decide on their own allegiances and destinies. I will not speak for them nor make a commitment on behalf of the committee."

The Guest displayed no expressions on his face. No human expression was adequate to convey the depth of his thoughts. No human emotion came to him either, for he was not human, much as he enjoyed masquerading as one.

"This is what I will be doing: I will be raising an army to fight this war. Given what I am, it will be easy for me. I had come here tonight to find out if the ancient ones will be standing with me, or against me. This I know for a fact—there will be no neutral parties, no fence-sitters in this war. There will be casualties. This is what is to come."

The Guest stood up and vanished on the spot. There was no fading, no compression to a single point, no puff of smoke, no vortexes, no fanfare. Emptiness emerged where he stood, as if the spot had never been occupied.

4

WAR GAMES

It was a cloudy day for once. A slight breeze caressed the trees and the animals and the activity that thronged Pulau Tekong, rising and dipping like fingers flitting across the keys of a grand piano. Marie Rose took a deep breath and inhaled the smells of the forest, although, technically, as a ghost she did not need to breathe. She rested her head on gnarled tree roots that were protruding slightly above the ground and gripping the earth like claws of a chimera. Weak sunlight found their way through the map of swaying leaves that dappled her face, creating playful shadows that danced on her porcelain skin. She found peace in the jungle, a familiar place that embraced her as a home would. Marie Rose felt with a sudden clarity of realisation that if she concentrated hard enough, she could by the force of her will alone quite simply cease the difficult business of existence; slip away quietly from reality and meld into the forest—no more unnaturally than an ice cube returning to water.

But the day was a beautiful one and she felt more buoyant than melancholic. She closed her eyes and listened to the music of the birds. She could recognise each of the distinctive songs of the mangrove blue flycatcher, the broadbill, the blue-naped monarch, the mangrove whistler, the sunbird. She could not communicate with them, but she knew that they were aware of her and were generally cordial towards her. Sometimes she brought stolen food from human dwellings for them. The company of birds was a small consolation for the aching loneliness Marie Rose often felt.

Against Grandmother Yang's sage advice, Marie Rose headed to the place where she knew she would find a kindly face. Someone to look at her and to meet her eyes. Someone she could pretend was a friend.

Marie Rose saw Leonard before he saw her. She picked out his face in a sea of recruits. He had a look of severity when he was concentrating on something. The soldiers stood at attention, listening to instructions rattled off by their platoon sergeant. They were about to begin the Standard Obstacle Course drill, which consisted of twelve stations simulating an urban combat terrain. Marie Rose had watched thousands of SOC runs by thousands of recruits over the years. But she had never tried it herself. *Why not? Why not today?* She grinned and stretched her long lithe limbs like a cat in the sun.

"Oh, hey, Leonard! What a coincidence seeing you here!" she said cheerfully as she vaulted herself across the low wall at the same time as Leonard did. She affected an expression of pleasant surprise, as if they had bumped into one another on a lovely morning stroll in the park.

Leonard groaned inwardly as he ignored her, blinking away the sweat that was trickling down from beneath his helmet into his right eye. His section had just been ordered by their sergeant to do twenty push-ups right before starting the SOC circuit in their full battle order, encumbered by filled water bottles, with their trusty rifles banging against their bones. A talkative ghost was the last thing he needed to get through his SOC in good timing.

"Nice day for a workout, isn't it? Really wakes you up and refreshes your soul," Marie Rose chatted conversationally as they leaped from one stepping stone to another in tandem like jive dancers in a smoky 1950s bar. Marie Rose was wearing her favourite swing skirt that bloomed around her like a blossom when she spun around. They leaped and ducked the rubble, two little frogs in a lotus pond.

"I've been thinking about your Ma-Mah," Marie Rose said as they crawled into the small tunnel. Somehow, defying all laws of physics, she was able to fit in right beside him in the tiny enclosed space. The tunnel echoed with Leonard's laboured breathing as he struggled to move as fast as he could with all the paraphernalia strapped to him. His helmet felt like a vice on his head, squeezing out any semblance of coherent thought.

Marie Rose kept up with him effortlessly, uncannily managing to stay right beside him all the time as they climbed the low rope, jumped over ditches, and crept around the edges of faux architecture.

"Nothing in this world lasts forever. Not even ghosts. She probably faded away because it was time for her to go. Because she felt ready to let you grow up now," Marie Rose bit her lip at the small white lie, tottering a little on the Apex ladder as she momentarily lost her concentration.

Concerned, Leonard's arm shot out despite himself and grabbed hold of her arm. They had ascended to the peak of the triangular Apex ladder, its rungs consisting of horizontal logs with huge gaps between them. It was at a great height off the ground. Catching his folly, he shook his head and rolled his eyes.

"What am I thinking? Worried about a ghost falling off the Apex ladder? I should worry for myself instead," he mumbled tersely, bracing himself slightly for the descent of the ladder and clasped his rifle closer to him so it would stop thwacking his body distractingly. Never had four kilograms worth of matter felt heavier and more damningly cumbersome.

Leonard charged at the remaining distances of terraces and completed the SOC with a final burst of energy. Utterly winded, he tried to catch his breath as Marie Rose continued to follow him like a little shadow, her steps light and effortless. He finally looked her in the eyes after drinking his fill from the bottle that he had carried up and down the obstacle course.

"Marie Rose, thank you for telling me about my Ma-Mah," he said seriously. "I'm just glad she is at peace now, wherever she is. That's all I hope for."

Marie Rose lowered her lashes, disconcerted. She hoped that she had done the right thing. She quickly stashed the uncomfortable thoughts to the back of her mind. She had had fun going through the obstacle course by Leonard's side. She savoured how exhilarating it had felt to shimmy up the low rope like a little monkey, flee down the steep steps made of logs on her tiptoes, and run the last length of distance in a maddened, exalted sprint. She felt almost alive, as if she knew what it was like to be afraid that her next breath might be her last.

These were disturbing, unusual thoughts. Marie Rose rubbed her nose absently, depositing a huge smear of mud on it. Leonard stared at the mud splattered on her face and on her pretty silk blouse with the dainty rounded collars. He felt a hysterical laugh bubbling up from deep within him, the laugh of a madman. He had just completed his SOC, in good timing, with a meddlesome, loquacious ghost by his side.

A surge of unexpected but monumental happiness rose in his chest. *Life could be worse*, he thought.

Against her better judgment, Marie Rose began to accompany Leonard for every aspect of his basic military training. She was beside him, cheering unnecessarily, as he trained for his Individual Physical Proficiency Test. She shadowed him silently as he and his team mates carried out elaborate drills for urban operations. She lay beside him as he stared up at the stars during his field camp, trying to fall asleep in his shell scrape with the whine of mosquitoes in his ears.

She did not speak to him much during the day, only answering when he wished to talk to her. She was content to go through the training activities with him, as if she were training to be a soldier too. She learned to do push-ups the way men did them. She learned how to disassemble a rifle, clean its parts, and put them all back together again. She learned to polish boots so hard they shone like a mirror. She learned how to fold military fatigues so that the name tags sat neatly, front-facing, when they were placed in the metal cabinets in the bunk. She learned how to throw a grenade. She learned how to put together a field pack. She learned how to eat combat rations straight from the olive green plastic packaging. She learned the different parade commands shouted in Malay and amused herself by following them along with the regiment. It was like a dance.

Most dangerously, she learned how to be a friend. She learned how to commiserate, how to sense the emotions of another without words exchanged, how to convey support in silence, how to share food and exchange stories, how to laugh at jokes at her expense. Some days, she felt so human it scared her. She could almost imagine that she felt physical pain when Leonard did, that she felt heat injury creeping up on her during long, seemingly endless route marches, that she felt simple joy in raising her voice to join others in belting out timeworn military songs.

But unlike the others, she could not book out of camp when they did. She had no family to return to at the end of the week. She had no one who wrote letters of encouragement to her, to be read during the culmination of field camp. She had no one who would remember her if she melted into the forest and never returned.

Marie Rose was walking a minefield, and it was only halfway through when she came to the jarring realisation that turning back would now be just as dangerous as moving forward.

~*~

Gradually, Leonard could no longer remember what it felt like to walk around Tekong without Marie Rose by his side. She proved to be a loyal companion, mostly quiet, and always invisible to everyone else. The inexplicable joy she displayed in tackling every single training activity—as though she were flinging every ounce of sincere effort contained within her small body at the task at hand—was extremely infectious. With her little feline winks and goading smiles, she coyly baited his bravado and competitive spirit as they trained together; pushing him to go faster, harder, stronger; driving him to achieve beyond what he would have imagined himself to be capable of.

Never one to endure the thought of losing to a girl, even one who was merely a ghost, Leonard began to excel at many of the training activities. She was unerringly there to cheer on his small successes and to offer whispers of encouragement when he faltered. His instructors silently noted his potential for command.

"Kinda hoping against hope but… I really wish to get selected for Officer Cadet School," Leonard whispered, trying not to wake any of his sleeping bunkmates, as Marie Rose lounged at the corner of his bunk bed.

He pictured the officers' commissioning parade in his mind's eye: rows of soldiers clad in the crisp, white Number 1 uniform, with its smart gold buttons, high peaked cap, and single red stripe running down its pant leg. He pictured his mother getting off of the sweat-stained mattress on the floor of their apartment, dressing herself in her old favourite floral blouse and navy blue skirt, coming to watch him march and cheer and throw his cap in the air alongside his friends. He pictured her fastening the lieutenant's epaulette on his shoulder, smiling at him with pride in her eyes.

Leonard shook his head, as though he could physically expel the fantasies from his mind. His mother no longer wore sweet, high-necked floral blouses and knee-length skirts. She got dressed up only to slip out late at night to walk the streets of Geylang. She had probably forgotten how to smile.

Marie Rose watched Leonard's face closely as he struggled to drag himself from the quicksand pull of self-pity and regret. She knew from her years of experience at Tekong that

Leonard was a most suitable choice. His peers and instructors liked him. He was honest, hard-working, and performed his duties uncomplainingly. He got along well with everyone. He had even grown to *look* the part of a commanding officer—a heavy brow, eyes that narrowed with intensity and concentration, angular jaw bones jutting jauntily from a face that had lost its boyish chubbiness. A man's face.

Despite herself, Marie Rose blushed a little. A ghost had no blood, but she had spent so much time with humans the past months, she had unconsciously picked up many human quirks and idiosyncrasies. Heat flooded her face and she touched her cheek wonderingly, marvelling at the very real warmth that emanated from her skin.

"So, what do you think? Is it only a silly daydream?" Leonard asked, breaking into her reverie.

"Well, I do hope you get selected too. Of all people, you deserve it most," Marie Rose smiled. "You've worked so hard the past few months. I saw it all. For you, I will wish upon a star."

Leonard was moved by her touchingly girlish words. He had not known many girls in his childhood and was unaccustomed to her vulnerable innocence. "Thank you, Marie Rose," he said sincerely. "For all that you have done to help me. I can't imagine going through my training without you now. You are the star that I will now wish upon."

5

THE WRITING ON THE WALL

"Order in the courtroom please!" Lady Pontianak banged a stapler against the table top, impersonating a judge. The Grassroots Committee of Ghosts and Monsters was teeming with raised voices—hotly deliberating, debating, some outright arguing. The old ghosts and monsters of Singapore were divided on The Guest's indubitably divisive call to arms.

"He said that he could raise an army! What could it mean?"

"Are we *allowed* to create something out of nothing?"

"Will he *be* creating something out of nothing? Or something out of something?"

"Is he relying only on the existing ghosts and monsters in Singapore to fight his war? It's impossible! They who do not even bother to join the Grassroots Committee of Ghosts and Monsters... what makes him think that they would bother becoming *soldiers* in his war?"

"Is he thinking of bringing *foreign talent* into Singapore to fight this war? Overseas ghosts and monsters. What if he is merely a foreign agitator, someone who doesn't have a stake in this land? Someone who will enable spirits from other countries to rule over *us*! This is a coup, that's what it is!"

The last ringing interjection by Auntie Chin echoed like a shriek, bouncing off the walls of the Grassroots Committee's meeting room. The members fell silent. They were growing afraid.

"Isn't it suspicious that we have never heard of this monster until only a few months ago? How could he have grown so powerful so quickly? He must be a foreigner, someone who was not born here at all," Uncle Bhuta mused. He addressed Lady Pontianak directly. All meeting members turned to her with beseeching expressions. They yearned for her help in making sense of The Guest, with his inexplicable existence and his inexplicable proposal.

Lady Pontianak sighed. She pinched the bridge of her nose for a moment. As though in accordance with her mood, messy tendrils of hair had escaped her usually impeccable up-do and hung limply at the side of her face.

"Look, everyone, a monster could grow silently in incubation for a long time before ever manifesting in the human world. In my view, The Guest is simply the apex of a swirling mass of fears that have been brewing for a long time, over decades of the country's evolution. We all know what an aberration the past half century has been. Life has undeniably become... fundamentally different from the old world we were so familiar with. Living and surviving alongside humans all these years... being embedded so deeply in their social fabric… I suppose we simply haven't been very sharp-eyed," Lady Pontianak ventured.

"I seriously don't believe that The Guest would be successful in achieving all that big talk. Spirits have never gone to war in the entire history of our existence. Never! The humans themselves do a good enough job of killing each other off. I can't believe he's serious, I just can't," the Eurasian vampire said emphatically.

"I am afraid of what I really feel, deep down, which is that… perhaps freedom for ghosts and monsters may be a worthy fight. We have been wretched and pathetic for so long," ventured the Monster Under the Bed. "But then… I go back to my home and look upon the faces of the little sleeping children, all snug and cosy in their little cots. I know then that I would never be able to bring myself to truly harm them. Or allow them to come to harm."

Many of the residential ghosts and monsters murmured their acquiescence.

"I don't feel such a strong attachment to individual visitors to my parks," said the Woman in the Red Dress. "But I suppose… sometimes… I do fancy myself as sort of a guardian of the parks. Of sorts. I keep watch over the visitors as they scurry around doing their little human things. Running round and round in circles making themselves all sweaty and breathless. Flying their ridiculous little drones. Queueing up outside mediocre restaurants in the evening humidity all bitten by mosquitoes. I don't know. I suppose I feel like a protective mother hen. Of sorts."

"I'm not certain that a Singapore run by ghosts and monsters would be much better than a Singapore run by humans. Sure, it would be more fun for us in the short term, I can imagine that. But would it be a good society? A just society? How can a society with humans as slaves be good and just?" argued the elder Marbles Child heatedly.

"I know that we Marbles Children come across as nothing more than frisky sprites who only care about video games and playthings. The fact is… we have been around for a long time too. We know that humans are intrinsically… different. Their creations are marvellous to behold. Some of them are terrible—evil, even—but many of them… just spectacularly beautiful. I very much believe that enslavement would cripple them. If enslavement were even possible, of course, *logistically speaking*," chimed in the younger Marbles Child.

"Yes, how can we make a decision when we don't know exactly what The Guest is planning to do? Who exactly will make up his army? What are the terms of his war? Is he going to fight fairly?" the Chinese vampire mused aloud. "We can't just throw our names into the ring, blindfolded. It's not fair for him to expect us to."

"I don't believe he would be fighting a fair battle," Lady Pontianak said softly, a faraway look coming into her eyes. "He reminds me of someone I once knew a long, long time ago. Someone cruel and indifferent. Victory will be sought at all costs. They will be no civilians, no neutral parties, no non-combatants. Everything will be up for grabs."

The meeting members looked uneasy. Lady Pontianak's

words did echo that of The Guest very closely. They knew then that she deeply understood the nature of what they were dealing with. And she had chosen to take the opposing side; the defending side, on the side of the humans. But many of the ghosts and monsters were apprehensive. They were simply not prepared to take up arms to protect humans. They barely felt capable of ensuring their own survival.

"Let's hope it never comes to that," Marie Rose said hopefully. "Maybe the war will never happen. Maybe, despite his self-assured certainty, he won't be able to raise a good enough army."

"That's what we all hope too," sighed Lady Pontianak. "But we have to begin to prepare ourselves, as though what The Guest said will indeed come to pass. There is too much to lose, for us to be caught off guard. Both for ourselves and for the humans under our care."

For the first time that evening, all the meeting members of the Grassroots Committee for Ghosts and Monsters nodded in agreement.

~*~

That evening, Leonard bore an unbearably grim countenance. He ate his meal silently, keeping to himself, ignoring the boisterous conversations and riotous laugher of his section mates around him. He stared off into space vacantly, a million thoughts grazing his mind. Marie Rose was beside herself with worry.

"What is it? What happened?" she exclaimed once the lights were doused that night. "I know that something's happened. Please tell me about it."

Leonard had flung an arm over his eyes and was lying on his bunk bed stiffly, as if straining with all his might to prevent any part of his body from touching the spot where Marie Rose usually sat. He was still lost in thought, his jaw clenched strenuously. When he finally lifted his arm from his eyes and glanced at Marie Rose, she thought she saw some tears. He studiously averted his gaze and stared at a spot on the ceiling.

"What's wrong, Leonard?" Marie Rose crept up to his elbow. She lay beside him and tentatively placed her head on the crook of his arm. She hesitated, holding her breath. She had never strayed from her usual spot at the foot of the bed during their night-time conversations. But this time, she sensed a deep wound within him, a vulnerability so palpable she felt she could hold it in her hands, warm and trembling like a small animal.

Leonard flinched, his whole body clenching like a fist about to strike. But he did not move away. He lay as he was, looking at the ceiling. Marie Rose listened to his breathing and followed the rise and fall of his chest with her eyes. She did not know what to do. She stayed where she was, her body turned on its side, inches away from his, her hair nestled against his arm.

Leonard half raised his other arm, as though reaching instinctively to rest a hand on her head, as one would pat a small dog. However he seemed to think better of it, arrested the motion, and placed his hand back on the mattress.

He gently nudged Marie Rose away as he pulled himself into a sitting position on his bed, arms crossed lightly on his knees.

"One of my section mates made a report to our commanders," he said after a long silence. "I don't know who it is. But he told them that he saw me frequently talking to myself or having conversations with empty space. My commanders ordered me to see the Medical Officer. And to undergo a psychiatric evaluation."

He pressed the heels of his palms against his eyes. "The MO asked me today if I was seeing things that nobody else saw. Or heard things that nobody else did. If I had a history of hallucinations."

He suddenly freed his eyes from the prison of his hands and turned his gaze to Marie Rose. He stared hard at her, as though he were undergoing an optometric test. He squinted at her, covered one eye with one hand and then the other, and looked so hard that Marie Rose felt she would splinter into oblivion. His hand shot out and grabbed her arm, as it once did when they were standing side by side atop the Apex ladder, the breeze in their hair and the sun in their eyes.

"Are you real? Are you just a figment of my imagination? Do you really exist?" he whispered in despair, and let go of her arm as abruptly as he had held it. "Is there such a thing as a ghost? Did I imagine it all? My Ma-Mah all those years... Perhaps it was such a good story I told myself that I just started to believe it. Perhaps my mother did take care of me after all. Perhaps we managed between ourselves to keep alive after my father left, somehow. There *was* no silent, kindly grandmother ghost fussing over me, loading the washing machine, folding my clothes, preparing dinner, listening to how my day had gone. Perhaps it was really all in my head, a pathetic hallucination."

He spat out the last word as though it were a curse. Marie Rose was taken aback. She did not have much experience on the subject of psychiatry or hallucinations. She had heard recruits jokingly insult each other: "*Siao* ah!"… "Crazy!"… But she did not realise how little she understood what sanity or insanity really meant to humans.

"Leonard, I… I don't know about your Ma-Mah. But I *think* I am real… I mean, here I am, talking to you… and you… talking back to me…" Marie Rose trailed off. She suddenly felt a little dizzy. She had never contemplated her own reality.

Marie Rose backed away from Leonard, retreating into her corner. She felt extremely frightened and disoriented. She could feel her grip on the world wavering. A prickling sensation of danger came over her, black and overwhelming.

"I'm going to go now. I'll catch you another time. Try to get some sleep, okay?" she sputtered, climbing down the bunk bed as fast as she could.

~*~

Several days wafted by. Marie Rose stopped showing up for Leonard's training. Her absence nagged at him, as though it were incontrovertible proof that she was indeed merely a concoction of a diseased mind.

Leonard hauled himself to his scheduled psychiatric evaluation like a condemned man stumbling to the guillotine. Dread rushed in to fill up every space in his numb, rattling skull. He was determined not to have his Physical Employment Status downgraded, not to allow the past few months of exertion and struggle swirl down the drain. Even at the cost of betraying his integrity.

The psychiatric evaluation session flew by in a blur of solicitous questions from a kindly, probing doctor, and the stumbling lies that tumbled from his mouth almost with a will of their own.

No, he did not see things that other people could not.

No, he did not hear things that other people could not.

Yes, sometimes he did have quite a bad habit of talking to himself—it's nothing really, just a lingering childhood remnant of praying aloud in nerve-wracking situations; it helps to clarify his thoughts; he's working on reducing it so as not to distract others; it's nothing, it's nothing; just a bad habit, a silly old bad habit.

Having put on his best performance of incontestable sanity, Leonard positively sprinted away from the hospital as a man chased by hounds snapping at his heels would.

I'm not crazy… I'm not crazy… I'm not crazy… Leonard chanted in his head feverishly, staggering blindly onto his bus and making the long commute back to Tekong.

Unfortunately, the conviction of his own sanity slowly slid away from him; a previously unperceived shroud that now slipped silkenly off the mien of his reality, revealing to him a strange, unfamiliar landscape.

Perfectly ordinary sounds began to feel all too loud and too tinny at the same time, stomping on his twitchy ear drums. Colours suddenly appeared too bright, too gaudy. There were moments when he looked at a friend's laugh and time seemed to slow—a whooshing sensation flooded his ears, the skin on his head felt too tight for his skull, the otherwise innocent laughter of his friend seemed to stretch and gape like that of a funhouse clown, manic and unfamiliar and dangerous.

He felt that his mind was disintegrating and he could do nothing to stop it. The world took on a patina of unrealness. Speaking was an immense effort, as though he were an actor launching into a soliloquy… and promptly forgetting his lines just as he opened his mouth. His heart seemed to spasm and seize randomly, with no relation whatsoever to what was happening at the moment.

He was certain that the others could sense his descent into craziness, certain that they despised him and disdained him. As he progressively withdrew into himself, his thoughts began to feel too loud in his own head—foreign, even. Like a stranger's voice, but inside his head. Alarmed at the sheen of distortion settling on his world, he started to scrutinise his inner monologue and felt increasingly detached from it.

Am I hearing voices in my head? Is this me speaking to myself? Am I talking to myself? Have I been talking to myself all this time?

He had never felt more frightened in his life.

~*~

THERE ARE VOICES IN MY HEAD. A clear, indisputable statement exploded across Leonard's consciousness, nearly bringing him to his knees.

He was merely taking a shower, lathering shampoo on his head, just like any other evening, when all of a sudden, his legs simply refused to hold up his body anymore. He came crashing down to the indifferent tiles. Shivering violently, his teeth chattered as though he had just emerged from the freezing cold water of a tossing ocean. He became aware that his heart—that traitorous organ, that had endured kilometres of route marches in the sun, that had faithfully brought his body to safety through bursts of running and jumping and diving, that had worked diligently all his life without demanding his conscious scrutiny or awareness— had suddenly decided to announce its presence loudly and vehemently.

In fact, his heart was beating so fast that Leonard was sure he would pass out. He placed his palm on his chest and felt the racing, rabbity pulse against his hand. Perhaps he was going to have a heart attack. In a flurry of irrational thoughts, he was seized by a conviction not to have his heart attack as he were, naked in a shower stall with shampoo still in his hair.

Before his heart could give out, he raced through the remaining motions of his shower and dried himself vigorously with his towel. On came his shorts and T-shirt, restoring his dignity.

Now, he was ready to drop dead from his heart attack.

Still breathing as heavily as though he had just completed a 2.4-kilometre run, Leonard leaned his forearm against the door of the shower stall and rested his head wearily on it. He listened as the voices in the toilet gradually faded. Most of the recruits had noisily finished their washing up and were leaving in dribs and drabs.

Please, let them all leave before you stop working, Leonard implored his heart silently. *Just a little while more, then I will open this door, and then we can have the heart attack.* It was way too embarrassing to have a heart attack right in the midst of all this raucous, cheerful activity. It was so inappropriate.

Finally, silence reigned in the toilet and the last of the recruits tramped out the door, chattering inanely of book-out plans and girlfriends and video games. Leonard unlocked the shower stall and spilled into the brighter light of the sinks and the mirrors and plastic dispenser still oozing green soap. He was still breathing very rapidly, his heartbeat way too loud and too fast to be normal. There was tension in his chest and he was not sure if he imagined some vague pain radiating slowly out from the flesh directly above his heart.

Lightheaded and unsteady on his feet, Leonard clutched a nearby sink desperately for support. He waited for his heart to stop beating, for his vision to fill with black constellations of stars, for *anything* to happen, anything but this agonising confusion, this unbearable infinite moment of bewilderment.

He placed his hand on his chest again, measuring his heartbeat. It seemed to be getting closer and closer to the surface of his chest, as if his heart was going to fly out of his body. Groaning, he lowered his head to the sink and gulped in large quantities of air like a drowning man breaking the surface of the sea.

But the sea was faraway, and there was nothing here but white tiles and fluorescent light and his pale, sweaty reflection in the mirror. Leonard felt overcome by the waves of anxiety.

"So this is how it will end for me? Dying here in a shabby toilet in Tekong?" he said aloud, startling himself with his trembling, slightly shrill voice. He suddenly felt unbearably alone and afraid. To his abject horror and shame, tears stung at his eyes.

"If I'm going to die of a heart attack, I will NOT be afraid of it!" he half yelled, the tears breaking free of their tenuous bonds and streaming down his face with wild abandon.

Just at that moment, a voice sounded.

"You are NOT going to die," Marie Rose said severely.

Leonard dashed the tears from his eyes with an angry, embarrassed swipe of his hands. He looked up.

Marie Rose had hopped up onto the sink next to him

and perched herself on it casually, legs crossed neatly at the ankles, palms supporting her weight.

"Leonard Liu," she said. "I am no psychiatrist, but if there's anything in the world I know most, it is *fear*."

She jumped down from the sink and took hold of his hand. "Trust me. I am a ghost. Fear is my area of expertise. These sensations you are feeling now… they have a name. It is only fear. Sheer, dumb, physical, animal fear. It is fear turned against your own mind."

Leonard was still breathing raggedly. He held her hand as if his life depended on it. "But my heart is beating abnormally fast… I'm quite sure I'm going to die of a heart attack…"

"No," Marie Rose cut in brusquely. "It's just a panic attack. I know it feels really uncomfortable right now, but it is NOT dangerous. Just think of it as a… muscle cramp. Searingly painful right now, but it will be over in a minute."

A tender memory flashed unbidden: Him rolling around on the ground, clutching his calf as a muscle cramp held it in its excruciating grip, while Marie Rose also rolled about beside him, laughing and seizing the opportunity to tickle his ribs wickedly as he groaned in pain.

She placed her small hand on the middle of his chest. "Keep breathing. Focus on your breathing. There's nothing in this moment except your breathing."

Leonard closed his eyes and felt his wretched, shaky breaths huffing in and out of his body in short sharp bursts.

"Look at me," Marie Rose shook his shoulder. "Slowly.

Breathe slowly. Your life is not in danger. Inhale slowly through your nose and exhale slower out your mouth."

Leonard did as he was told. His breathing began to slow. Marie Rose moved her hand from his chest to his stomach.

"Fill your breath *here*. Not in your chest. Imagine expanding your stomach full of air like a balloon as you inhale, and deflating it as you exhale," she instructed.

Leonard struggled a little with the unfamiliar feeling but he tried his best. Soon, Marie Rose's hand was moving up and down slowly and rhythmically as his stomach rose and fell in tandem with his breaths.

"Leonard..." she said softly. "You are not crazy, you hear me? Madmen do not ask themselves if they are mad. The world makes perfect sense to them. *You* are only afraid. And I understand that now. Come. Will you make me a promise? And I will make a promise to you too."

"What is it?" Leonard asked shakily. He was leaning against the sink, still holding on to Marie Rose's hand.

"Stop worrying about seeing ghosts anymore. Stop worrying about sanity and insanity. It doesn't mean anything. You are strong and brave and loyal, as I have witnessed myself. You stepped up to lead when nobody else wanted to. You spoke up on behalf of the section when all were mute. You helped your team mates when they faltered. You are a steady friend, a worthy soldier, a budding commander. I believe in you," Marie Rose said emphatically. "A duck who quacks like a duck and looks like a duck and walks like a duck is a duck. He does not need to worry about sanity or insanity. You are a good person and a leader of men. Don't stop being the Leonard I know."

Leonard stared at her steadily. He could feel pinpricks at the back of his eyes—errant tears threatening to return again. He felt so ashamed of his weakness, his cowardice.

"Marie Rose… I don't know if I can promise you that…" he said falteringly.

"You can," she replied. "You can. Because here is my promise to you. I will never appear to you again. I will ensure that all the ghosts and monsters of Tekong will stay away from you. You will complete the rest of your basic military training in peace. This I promise you."

Slowly, she pulled her hand out of his big, warm grasp. She hurried away, careful to turn her head so he would not see the tears that had sprung up in her own eyes.

"Marie Rose… wait…" Leonard started after her.

She ran.

Swinging the door open forcefully, she streamed out of the toilet, turned a corner, and switched off her physical appearance.

Leonard's footsteps sounded behind her as he wrenched the door open again and scanned the surroundings hurriedly. He saw nothing.

Marie Rose sat in a pool of shadows, invisible, as she buried her face in her knees and sobbed with abandon.

6

BLOOD AND TEARS

Life went on. Leonard and his fellow recruits began to prepare for their long-awaited Passing Out Parade, which officially signified the successful completion of their basic military training course. Despite the flurry of activity, Leonard could not ignore the gnawing guilt and emptiness that ate at him. To make matters worse, the long shadow of the panic attack he had experienced haunted him and elicited from him quakes of fear like no ghost ever had.

Suppose I have a panic attack again here, he thought as they endured ceaseless marching drills in the parade square.

And here? How dreadful it would be. At the start of a long route march.

What if it happens now? At the cookhouse, having lunch, squeezed in the middle of hundreds of soldiers.

A panic attack would be horrendously embarrassing now. At the inter-company sports day, a day of athletic showiness and striving for glory to one's "coy".

There was no escaping the tendrils of lingering fear, a phantom limb that ached and itched and tingled. Strong, brave, loyal Leonard, effortless laughter, carefree days... these receded into the distant territory of the past: the lost, irretrievable and unchangeable past, the land of no return. The present was miserable and the future seemed bleak.

Just how do I get out of this despicable slump? How do I pull myself together? Leonard thought to himself despondently, numbly packing his belongings in preparation for his final days at Tekong.

Everywhere he went, he looked for Marie Rose.

In his mind's eye, he saw her everywhere.

The cookhouse. Smiling at him across the table, trying to provoke an answering grin with her silly antics—her little finger up his unsuspecting buddy's nose, a spooky wobble of their Milo mugs after the sun had set, her uncannily accurate impersonation of his *encik* as she stood right behind the good man himself.

The parade square. Her ridiculous girly marching. Her earnestly stern salute, small hand snapping to her temple and back down to her side. Her full skirts rustling around her thighs as she pivoted and stamped and turned with all the grace of a prima ballerina.

Area cleaning. Sitting atop his back as he was down on his hands and knees scrubbing the floors with a Scotch-Brite, somehow weighing no more than a feather. Humming her creepy vintage Chinese songs and sticking out her tongue when he shushed her urgently.

The bunk. Her spot at the corner of his bed. Her toes buried in his scratchy blanket. Her fingers curled around the metal ladder as she climbed up and down every night, keeping up her studious illusion of humanness.

Stand by area. Her laughing face shaking with mischief, half-buried in her hands, as she watched the platoon sergeant yell at a perplexed recruit whose impeccable bed had been inexplicably un-made by unseen forces when his back was turned.

He missed her. He craved the shy, tentative smile that lit up her face when she met his eyes. He wanted her to place her hand on his abdomen again as he concentrated on breathing slowly in and out. He needed her unexpected certainty and firm advice on how to combat fear and anxiety.

Where is she? He wondered if she was still around, albeit invisible to him now like the rest of them. He wondered if she watched out for him, if she worried about him. He wondered if she even thought about him.

What do you want from her? A sobering thought arose. *What is it, do you want to hold her hand, kiss her, ask her to be your girlfriend? She is a ghost, for heaven's sake! How would that work out? Or do you intend to persuade her to come back to the main land with you, to live with you, and watch over you, until you get tired of her? Hang around aimlessly as you move on with your life? Would she be happy? To follow you around forever like a slavish lapdog, as you go on to fall in love with another, kiss another, wed another? Just what do you want from her, you hateful wretch?*

Leonard despised himself. So selfish, so stupid. Perhaps

it was best that they parted ways as they did. She was a Tekong ghost, born to the island, belonging to the island. He was merely a visitor, a guest passing by. He would complete his training, receive his vocational posting, and move on. Just like all other recruits have done before him, and would do after him. She would be here to witness it all. From now to eternity.

He could barely suppress the despair that rose within him like a tidal wave, a despondency that could not be reasoned away. He wanted to see her one last time. To say goodbye, to say thank you, to say that he never once regretted being able to see her. To tell her she was possibly the best friend he ever had, and would ever have. To have her know that she made him a better man.

A proper farewell. It was what he owed to her.

Midnight came. The witching hour. The playtime of ghosts and spirits and monsters. Leonard made his way to their usual toilet and barred the door with a broom.

"Marie Rose!" he whispered, feeling slightly foolish in the empty space. "Marie Rose, come out, please, I need to talk to you."

He went to the window and whispered the same words, hoping the wind would carry them to her. He sang the ridiculous eerie 1950s songs about love and loss that she so adored, his voice hoarse and crackly. He tapped her usual little plaintive melody on the window panes with his nails, as she often did to scare the men.

No Marie Rose.

The toilet was as reverently silent as a pharaoh's tomb. Leonard sighed.

"Marie Rose, please just come out. I will be leaving Tekong soon and I don't know if I will ever be able to return again. I just want to see you one last time," Leonard pleaded to the empty air.

He almost laughed aloud at the irony of it all. He was, indeed, now talking to himself, talking to empty space—exactly what his section mate had accused of him. Well, guilty as charged.

He paced around the toilet, thinking hard. He should have expected that Marie Rose would be so stubbornly stoic in keeping a promise. He expected no less of someone like her.

Leonard rested his hand on one of the sinks, recalling with a plummeting feeling in his stomach the terrible panic attack he had struggled through at that very spot. His body remembered the incident. Muscles tensed. His traitorous heart began to clamour for attention once more, pounding rapidly, throbbing in his ears. Gulping desperately, he tried to remember Marie Rose's calming hands, her instructions, her reassurances.

Slowly through the nose, and even more slowly out the mouth.

An idea came to him.

She had come to him when he last had the panic attack.

She had come to help him even though she had avoided him for days before the incident. She had cared.

Bracing himself, Leonard prepared to induce in himself the grandmother of all panic attacks. He squeezed his eyes shut and modified his breathing, huffing in and out at a harried rate. He imagined himself panting like a dog after a 2.4-kilometre run. He doubled over, clasped the edge of the sink, and flung an arm to his stomach. He grunted and groaned, convincing himself that something terrible was happening, that he was going to die just that very second.

Panic! Panic! I am so panicked! he told himself in his mind.

It sounded silly, like a stand-up comedian's punchline. Or a little advertising jingle.

Panic! Panic! I am so panicked!

The harder he tried to induce a panic attack, the more he realised that he could not. He could not make himself panicky. The waves of anxiety began to subside even as he deliberately took quicker and shorter breaths, even as he laser-focused on the sensation of his heart beating in his ribcage, even as he made straining, anguished sounds akin to those typically accompanying the expulsion of particularly stubborn poop. The ridiculousness of it all dawned on him and everything suddenly seemed unbearably funny.

Panic! Panic! I am so panicked! I am going to die from being so panicked!

For the first time in days, the very real and tangible fear that had dug its claws into him since his first panic attack began to subside. He felt light, buoyant, lucid. Here he was, going through the motions of a full-blown panic attack, his heart still pounding very quickly, his breathing unbelievably fast… but he was alright. He was fine. Nothing dangerous was happening. His heart did not burst out of his chest cavity in outright mutiny. He did not drop dead on the tiles. He felt a little light-headed, but he did not faint. He could not make himself faint.

Trying to induce a panic attack was tiring work.

He stood up straight for a moment and stretched his back out. It made a soft *krick* sound as he rolled out the tension.

Might as well stretch out my neck too, he thought and rolled his head around his shoulders slowly, as though warming up for the daily morning physical training. *Krick, krick.*

He breathed in and out deeply, concentrating on the sensation of the air entering his nostrils and then out again. He placed his hand on his stomach and felt the balloon-like inflation and deflation as he drew his breath right down to his diaphragm.

Calm and peace settled over him; a woollen sweater on a rainy day. He imagined the warmth of Marie Rose's hands. Her slightly brown eyes. Her paranormal freckles. Her smile.

Leonard opened his eyes.

He was still alone. Nothing disturbed the plain, dingy toilet. The air was quiet and stagnant. It was a warm night, with no breeze, no moon in the sky, no song, no Marie Rose.

Leonard sighed deeply. He was getting weary. He was convinced that Marie Rose was nowhere near. Perhaps she had moved on to haunt another company now. Rattling windows in some other block, singing sweetly in some other poor bloke's ear.

He removed the broom from the door handle and left. Perhaps it was for the best. She was a ghost and he was a mortal. There was nothing he could want of her, nor she of him. The world was cleaved into its two irreconcilable halves—the natural and the supernatural. And that was the end of that.

The Passing Out Parade came and went. It felt bittersweet, without Marie Rose celebrating by his side. After all, the two of them had gone through much of the entire training programme together. Leonard felt she deserved to be there, to be proclaimed a full-fledged soldier alongside him. A dull ache had taken up residence within him, a deep sense of unease and incompletion. He knew he had to see her one last time before he left Pulau Tekong for good.

As his fellow section mates jubilantly swarmed their bunk after the parade, grabbing their neatly packed belongings and cleaning out the cabinets like a throng of locusts, he set out to look for Marie Rose again. Unlike most, he had no family members waiting to accompany him home. There was no one there to slap him on the back with hearty congratulations, to pose beside him in commemorative photographs, to tell him how proud they were of him. His mother's absence was expected, but painful nonetheless.

Leonard traipsed around the places that had become familiar to him over the course of the few months in Tekong. He looked everywhere they had been to together, calling her name softly. He knew he was being foolish, looking for her as if she were some stray cat or misplaced object, expecting to find her in some specific location. Despite the foolishness, he still searched anyway, hoping that his pitiful ghost-like wandering would somehow attract her attention and bring her back to him. As he combed the place methodically, he realised that he did not know what he would even say to her, if and when he found her at all. Words felt pitifully inadequate in encapsulating the roiling tumult of emotions and confused desires that transfixed him.

Good bye.
Come with me.
Farewell forever.
Come see me again.
Good bye.
Not good bye.
Farewell.
Please stay with me for a while longer.

He sighed. What a sorry, pathetic creature he was. He wanted to talk to Marie Rose, ask her for her advice. He wanted her to sit at the foot of his bed once again, recounting the adventures of the day and whispering soothing nonsense. He wanted to grab her by her thin, fragile shoulders and shake her, yelling, "How could you bear to abandon me? How could you leave just like that?" Yet he knew that he would do precisely the same to her in time.

He drifted and he sighed. The irony of his situation was not lost on him. He was now the woeful, wandering spirit in the ghost stories, mournfully looking for something that was lost to him forever.

How *did* ghosts come about anyway? He had asked Marie Rose once before, but she had given him a vague, short reply before turning to more pressing matters, such as rearranging the contents of his buddy's cabinet and sneaking rocks into his field pack. Something about being born of fear and being sustained by fear.

He thought of his Ma-Mah. How did ghosts pass away? What was the reason for them passing away? He had initially thought that it was his offerings that had sustained her. If not, then what did? Did they simply just fade away naturally, as Marie Rose had once implied? As a natural course of events, like the turn of the seasons or the orbits of the heavenly bodies?

His head hurt to contemplate these questions. He had not even started on the more difficult questions about the fundamental nature of reality (*whose reality?*). Philosophy was not his strong suit.

Marie Rose would know what to say. She would have good-enough answers to these questions. Heavens, how he missed her.

Leonard rubbed his face with his palms. When had he

become a mawkish protagonist in a romance novel? The leading man in a chick flick?

Just then, he pictured himself caricatured in a large blown-up movie poster, caught in the moment of leaning in for a chaste kiss with a swooning Marie Rose. He had the urge to laugh and quickly stifled it. Marie Rose would laugh at that too. He knew she would.

He was so engrossed in his own thoughts that he did not realise that night had fallen. Unwilling to concede defeat, he slowed his steps and tried to come up with a strategy.

He had to do something dramatic. A grand gesture. That silly stray thought about romance novels and chick flicks had provided him with a spark of inspiration. Sure, he had no bouquets of roses or candles or chocolates among his measly possessions in Tekong. But he had one thing he was sure would get her attention—his mortality.

Leonard's belongings were the only ones left in his bunk. The room felt hollow, deserted. He quickly fished out his standard issue army jackknife. In the bright lights of the bunk, he felt exposed, vulnerable to scrutiny. He had to do this somewhere more secluded.

How about the most haunted place in Pulau Tekong?

He sifted through a rough mental catalogue of all the Tekong ghost stories he had been told over the years. Unfortunately, he had not been paying attention most of the time. Details were hazy. There might be a cemetery somewhere on Tekong. But he remembered Marie Rose once snorting derisively that cemeteries were, in fact, the least haunted places, for what need do ghosts and monsters have for dead humans? The dead could not prepare offerings, tell stories, feel frightened. So no, not the cemetery.

The mental catalogue flicked, page by page...

And he remembered. The infamous abandoned primary school. That would be perfect.

Marie Rose had once told him offhandedly, again in her typically vague fashion, the location of the abandoned primary school. Without hesitation, Leonard grabbed his flashlight and fled the bunk.

To his amazement, Leonard actually managed to find the place. The squat, modest building was almost crumbling. Rot and unidentified fungi engulfed much of what remained of the architecture. The blackened concrete had not heard footfall in decades. Leonard was glad for the strong beam of his flashlight. It would be most inconvenient to step on some decaying rat carcass underfoot, or walk into an unstable structure.

He tried not to think too much about it, but he hoped that no ghost or monster would conduct the jump-scare technique on him. He was not a fan of horror movies, nor did he enjoy a classic heart-pounding startle.

"Marie Rose? Are you here?" he asked. His voice sounded too loud in the isolated place. The darkness was oppressive. "Marie Rose, will you come see me? I have something to tell you."

The interior of the small one-storey edifice was furnished in the distinctive style of the bygone colonial era. He could imagine it being breezy and comfortable in its time.

"Hello? If anyone is here, could you tell Marie Rose that I'm looking for her? She's my friend. Please don't jump-scare me. It won't be worth your energy. I have what you would know as the 'third eye'. I won't be afraid of you," Leonard proclaimed to the empty building, feeling slightly foolish. He swung his flashlight this way and that, bracing himself for chance encounters.

"Marie Rose? If you're here, could you give a holler? I came all the way here to look for you," he called again. "But please don't jump-scare me. I might accidentally punch you if you do, okay? I just want to talk to you."

There was no answer. The place was dishearteningly silent and indeed abandoned. By both men and spirits. Leonard sighed.

He crouched to place his flashlight on the ground. The beam of light sliced a meagre, narrow path through the darkness. He took a deep breath, inflated his stomach, and stood up once more.

At this moment, he began to feel a little nervous. Jogging on the spot for a while, he shook out the tension in his hands and legs. He practiced the deep breathing techniques for a few minutes, one hand clasped lightly to his abdomen to feel the motions of his diaphragm.

It was now or never.

Leonard removed the jackknife from his pocket. He unsheathed the sharp blade and lifted it high in the air, like a magician showing an item to his audience and inviting them to check its ordinariness.

There was no audience. All was calm and silent, save for the hidden crickets in the grass imploring stridently outside the school.

Leonard took another deep breath.

"BY THE POWER OF MY MORTAL BLOOD I SUMMON YOU!" he yelled and brought the knife down upon his open palm. A deep gash opened up as his skin yielded to the sharp blade. His blood, appearing almost black in the darkness of the surroundings, welled up immediately.

Leonard kept his palm wide open and let the blood drip slowly, voluptuously, to the ground.

It dripped, and dripped, and dripped.

A minute or two of stillness.

And then.

"YOU IDIOT!" A female voice broke the silence. "LEONARD! You complete idiot! IT DOESN'T WORK THAT WAY!"

Finally, Marie Rose came running through a corridor from the depths of the building and rushed to Leonard's side. She had started to cry, her shoulders shaking, as she clutched at her cheeks where the tears gathered in rivulets.

"You are such an idiot!"

Marie Rose grabbed Leonard's bleeding hand and pressed fistfuls of her skirt into the wound. She kept pressure on the wound as hard as she could, willing all her strength and power and years into her clasp. Her entire body was shaking violently now as she wept. She held onto Leonard's hand with all her might.

"What were you thinking? Who told you to do this? This is the stupidest idea I have ever heard. Human blood is in no way any sort of sacrificial offering to spirits, you hear me? It doesn't work that way. You're such an idiot, you know that?" Marie Rose said in despair, her eyes finally lifting to meet Leonard's.

He smiled wanly. "It worked… it did work… you're here now, aren't you?"

His blood was soaking the fabric of her skirt. Marie Rose lifted her hand to examine the wound. Her tears continued to fall.

It was not as deep as it initially looked, but the bleeding had not stopped. Marie Rose was wracked with fear and despair. The tears fell from her downturned face directly onto his palm.

Leonard placed his other hand on Marie Rose's cheek. He gently turned her face up towards him. "It's okay, Marie Rose, I'll be fine. It's just a small cut," he whispered softly to her.

More tears fell on his palm as she stood numbly, still shuddering and heaving from vehement sobs. "Leonard, don't ever do something so stupid again. Please… I can't believe you hurt yourself."

Just then, there was a sharp intake of breath from Leonard as he suddenly flinched and raised his injured hand to his face for closer scrutiny.

His palm was empty.

"Marie Rose… look… the wound… it's… I don't know. It's gone," he said, marvelling at the smooth skin on his palm. His hand looked completely flawless, as if he had never cut it. He was befuddled. "What happened? Your tears…?"

Marie Rose looked down at his palm and then at the blood on her skirt, disconcerted. The gash had indeed disappeared. "I… I don't know what happened. I've never… my tears… I've never *healed* anything before," she stammered, brows furrowed in confusion.

She grabbed the flashlight lying on the ground and directed its beam at Leonard's palm. The wound was indeed gone, as though it never existed.

"It doesn't matter. Marie Rose, I've missed you so much." Leonard exhaled. "Did you know I've been looking all over for you? Did you care?"

Marie Rose started to cry all over again. "Of course I care! You big oaf! You idiot! I was trying to do what was the best for you. And now you came here, waving your big stupid bleeding paw, and I don't know what to do anymore." She broke into bouts of irrepressible sobbing, hiding her face in her hands.

Leonard gently lifted her hands away from her face and pulled her into an embrace.

"I'm so sorry, Marie Rose," he whispered into her hair. "I didn't mean to scare you. I'm alright. We're alright. Let's go outside and talk, okay?"

Marie Rose buried her face in the crook of his neck. The arms that held her were steady and unwavering. She wished she could stay in that moment, warm and safe and beloved, in perpetuity.

Now that Marie Rose was beside him, all words flew out of Leonard's head. He had no idea what to say. So they sat on a tree stump outside the abandoned school silently, as Leonard distractedly rubbed the spot on his palm where the gaping wound had been just minutes before.

Finally, Marie Rose broke the silence. "I'm sorry, Leonard. I know how hard you tried to look for me. But I also know that you have to leave this place soon. Most probably never to return. I thought it was better that we didn't continue to see each other again."

Leonard lifted his head at that. "Are you able to leave this island? You are able to, aren't you? I've heard you say that you've been to the mainland for a committee meeting."

Marie Rose sighed. "I can leave Tekong, but… only as a traveller. I can go to the mainland only as a guest. I was born to this place and I am bound to this place. It's hard for me to explain… but if I am away for too long, I will no longer be able to hold on to my existence. I literally have no presence on the mainland. No ties, no one to bear me. No one knows me there. No one has told my story there. My history, my self, my spirit… all belongs to Tekong. And there is nothing I can do to change it."

Leonard fell silent. A creeping realisation had dawned on him. An uncomfortable truth. He just suddenly *knew*. As if a factoid had dropped from the sky into his brain.

"So… that's how my Ma-Mah must have faded away," he said. "She must have tried to follow me to Tekong when I started my basic military training. To watch over me. She must not have understood. That it meant the end of her."

It was Marie Rose's turn to fall silent.

"There are many reasons why a ghost could cease to exist. Even we don't know all of them. But… I want you to know that ceasing to exist is not… harsh. For us, it's not difficult. It's not painful. It's not violent. There is only calm, and peace," she said, remembering the day in the forest. "If your Ma-Mah followed you, it was because she loved you. And she knew you loved her."

Leonard turned his head to gaze at her with a blistering intensity. "And you? Do you know?"

Marie Rose blinked. She lowered her lashes and looked down at her lap. The blood was now gone from her skirt, as if its colour had evaporated as well. She clasped and unclasped her fingers, intently avoiding his gaze.

Leonard started to speak again. "I came to look for you.

Because I wanted you to know. I... I am more than grateful for what you have done for me, for how much you have helped me. You very probably saved my life," Leonard said very softly. "And now, for the life of me, I can't find the right words to tell you how I feel. How I... a selfish and cowardly man... I still need your help. I still need you with me. But I don't have anything to offer you in return. I have nothing to give."

Marie Rose was gripping her own hands so hard her knuckles bones threatened to pierce through her skin. Her body froze with the awful anticipation, fervour, pain, and what else? She did not know. She had no idea what to say to Leonard in response. How to help him see what she felt for him.

So he continued speaking to her. "I know now that I can't ask you to come with me. That it would mean the end of you. But... could you... could you visit me? Once in a while, every time the moon is full." He smiled wryly at his own sentimental words. "Just as how you are able to visit the mainland to attend the committee meetings. Just a little water now and then, to keep this poor cactus alive."

Marie Rose raised her glistening eyes. "You do remember, don't you, that I'm not a human girl. I'm not a woman you can have and hold, till death do us part. I can't know if what you wish would do you more harm than good."

Leonard felt his heart constrict. Woefully, he was certain that this would be the moment it would finally mutiny and stop beating forever. He looked hard at Marie Rose, her tender beauty resplendent beneath the lonely night sky. He wanted to memorise every line of her body, every dip and curve and hollow. He wanted to disappear into the forest with her, hand in hand, never to be seen again.

"Is there no way?" he asked, his voice harsh with sorrow. "If this were a fairy tale, there would be some ancient, powerful sorceress we could go to. We would give her something in sacrifice. And she would turn you into a mortal girl, *my* mortal girl, to have and to hold, till death do us part."

Marie Rose held back her tears. "This is not a fairy tale," she whispered.

7

BOOTS ON THE GROUND

"This is a very crucial point in your lives together. A turning point. From now on, nothing will be the same again. The thought of your own lives will seem to pale in comparison to the over-riding concern for your little one. I'm sure you agree with me on this," the insurance agent said gravely to the young couple seated before him.

They both looked steeped in exhaustion, the smudges of purple-grey dark beneath their eyes. The young mother kept one hand on the pram as their cherubic newborn slept on soundly beneath its lowered hood, oblivious to the occasional roar of the coffee machine, clattering of utensils, and general background chatter of other customers in the coffee joint.

"I speak from my own experience, of course," the insurance agent said knowingly and somewhat vaguely. "The little bundle of joy now takes precedence over everything else. As parents, we want to do all that we can within our means to protect him."

The new parents nodded absently. *Protect him*. Of course, they would give anything, pay anything, to ensure that all eventualities were catered to, all risks smoothed over. The new baby was their world, their little angel: the pooping, puking, burping, howling, smiling and chirruping angel who dominated their lives now. It was a turning point. Nothing would be the same again.

"It's the perfect chance to take some time, review your portfolio, ensure you have everything you need to cover your new family's needs," the insurance agent cooed smoothly. "In fact, it's great that both of you are sitting down with me right now. Some people go their whole lives having their insurance policies collect dust in the highest cabinet in their homes, never reviewing them, never understanding what they have or what they are paying for, never taking the time to ensure that they have the coverage that they need. *Until it is too late.* The accident comes, the unexpected illness, the hospitalisation, the what-have-you. And then, it's too late when they realise that they have insufficient insurance coverage. That they have to empty their life savings, their *very retirement funds*, to tide them over."

The young father sighed and twirled his pen round and round his fingers. It was painful, imagining all the misfortunes and ills of this world that could befall their perfect little family. But it was a necessary pain, of course. It was the prudent thing to do. The savvy thing to do. Even if it means enduring the acute fear that came with picturing the unexpected death of… himself, or his wife, the only breadwinners and caretakers of their precious, precious little angel.

Or perhaps a sudden loss of income. That economic recession. An abrupt manpower cut in his industry. His wife's lack of higher educational qualifications. And there were the sheer brute accidents. A car accident. *Oh, many people do not know: driving is heinously more dangerous than hopping on an aeroplane. Can you imagine, five million traffic accidents is to twenty airline accidents on average per year.* No need to even get behind the wheel—simply walking on the pavement these days has you susceptible to being knocked down by an e-scooter, leaving you grievously and expensively injured, or dead, or worse, brain-dead. Brain-dead: hooked up to life support machines, beep, wife weeps, family decides to pull the plug, beep.

"As parents, we are responsible for making sure that our loved ones will still be able to go on with life without too much financial hardship even if we should most unfortunately pass on before our time. Would your wife be able to raise the baby on her own, financially speaking, should you go before your time?" the insurance agent addressed the young father, who shook his head. "I thought so too. Life insurance coverage is of utmost importance. Let me leave these documents for that to this side first. Afterwards, we can go over the calculations to reach an estimate of sufficient coverage based on your combined monthly salaries."

The insurance agent lifted a stack of papers from a larger stack and placed them emphatically on an empty spot on the table.

"Now, besides coverage in the event of loss of the parents'

lives, we also have to think for our children's well-being. Your baby may be perfectly healthy now, but sadly, children do have the chance of developing serious illnesses or get into accidents throughout the stages of their development. It's best to have some form of private health plan for the child, to augment the government's very basic Medishield Life coverage. I'll explain the options to you later so we can decide on the optimal level of coverage you feel is sufficient to protect your kid," the insurance agent explained.

Once more, he extracted a smaller stack of papers from the larger stack. The young parents were weary with anxiety. The young mother looked to her baby from time to time, her heart constricting at the sight of her little sleeping cherub. His little fingers were curled into a fist like the daintiest seashell.

"Besides planning for the eventualities in which they fall ill or get into accidents, many young parents also buy life insurance as a most valuable gift for their children. This is the perfect time for you to buy life insurance for him, whilst he is still young, free of existing health conditions and is hence most insurable. As you know, life insurance premiums only increase with age. Securing a plan for him now will ensure that he has a head-start in life. When he is all grown up, he will pay much lower insurance premiums than peers who only start buying life insurance then. Speaking of a head-start in life, many parents also use endowment funds as a smart saving tool to prepare for when the child goes to university." The insurance agent was talking faster and faster.

The young mother could barely keep up with the words that were spilling from his mouth like an overzealous waterfall. All that bounced around her head were a few hellish phrases. *In case he falls ill. In case he gets into an accident. In case he is hospitalised.* She glanced over at her sleeping son once more and felt she could burst into tears from the exhaustion and worry. Peaceful, uninterrupted sleep for her was a distant memory. She hoped that her husband was paying close attention to the insurance agent because she certainly was not. She imagined her baby's unbearably smooth, pink skin mangled in a horrific accident. She pictured it broken out in purple bumps and mottled lumps. She thought of her boss's hastily concealed irritation when she had first announced her pregnancy and her plans for her maternity leave. She thought of the frantic, desperate days that made up her life now— every action performed with the sole objective of keeping this little being alive.

The insurance agent was now talking about riders and gesticulating at colourful tables printed on glossy brochures. The young mother felt her eyes glazing over. She prayed that she would not keel over right at that moment. She took a huge sip of her cappuccino and glanced at her sleeping baby again. He had started to fidget slightly, kicking his small legs at an invisible foe. Could she hold back any enemy that comes for him in this life? Could she protect him against all the evil and ills of the world? Could she be the best mother that he deserves?

She thought about her husband's job. It required him

to travel frequently, despite her resentment about it. It had been difficult enough when they were merely newly-weds. She did not dare to imagine how she could possibly cope alone when he had to leave again for weeks on end. *Find another job,* she had pleaded. Surely there was something else out there that enabled him to come home to them every night of the year. But there was nothing else. *The job market is bad now. Nobody is hiring. I am lucky to even have this job.*

Despite the insurance agent's many doomsday predictions, she could barely bring herself to imagine her husband losing his job. Losing his life, yes. But losing his job… that would be a disaster for them both. How would they be able to cope for the time he would need to find another job? In her mind's eye, she saw herself as a cartoonish old crone dressed in grey rags, knocking on the door of a nebulous social services centre, clutching an emaciated baby to her chest. She pictured her breasts shrivelling up and refusing to give milk from lack of nutrition. She pictured her young son in one of his great purple fits, yelling with all the rage of a deity denied.

The insurance agent had now moved on to talking about insurance products that were good-to-haves, which *many young parents* have, which would *secure their future and give them peace of mind.* She closed her eyes again. She had agreed to her husband's suggestion to meet with the insurance agent because he had said that they needed the *peace of mind.* Somehow, listening to the agent's spiel disturbed her peace of mind more than ever. Fears of death, disease, unemployment, and poverty now crowded her head, each raising its voice louder and louder, jostling to be heard first.

Her husband's head was bent at an uncomfortable angle as he concentrated on the scrawls of numbers and equations that the insurance agent was now producing with great gusto. Figures on brochures were circled emphatically with markers. Little stars were drawn next to sentences of interest. Papers were dog-eared for future reference. The calculator was vigorously tapped at.

She struggled to focus on what the insurance agent was saying. She thanked the heavens for her husband's valiant attentiveness, for his reassuring hand on the back of her chair.

"Yes, I think that makes sense," she heard her husband saying and turning to look at her. "What do you think, dear? Should we go ahead with this?"

She nodded numbly, praying that he would not notice her distraction. "Yes, it sounds good. It sounds prudent."

"In that case, I'd just need both your signatures here… here… here… and here…" The insurance agent had very swiftly presented his tablet to them, pre-loaded with forms.

So many forms, she thought as they scrawled clumsily on the screen with the rubbery tip of the stylus over and over again.

Finally, it was over. The policies were signed. The annotated papers and brochures were slipped neatly into a folder bearing the insurance company's logo and handed to them for safekeeping. Exhortations to call on the insurance agent's services were made. The young mother sighed with relief as she turned to adjust her baby's blankets. The young father shook the insurance agent's hand perfunctorily and made some parting small talk about the state of the local public transportation.

None of them noticed as a supernatural event unfolded right beneath their very noses. Unseen to human eyes, the folder brimming with insurance policies began to smoulder. The smoke was midnight black and tinged with shimmer. Tendrils curled and danced as more and more dark smoke poured from the folder, forming a substantial cloud that hovered over the table for a moment. The smoke cloud opened eyes that sparkled, two diamonds in the dark. It began scuttling away from the table on tendrils that made provisional limbs—a strange, otherworldly crab-like creation of no ordinary circumstances. The creature melted into the stark shadows cast by the afternoon sun.

Also invisible to the eye, The Guest stood in the middle of the café, dressed in his favourite human skin, watching the birth of his first smoke demon. He raised his head and laughed for a long time, his white throat bared to an indifferent sun.

The army was raised with alarming speed. As promised, it was easy for The Guest, child to the contemporary fears of the people. He knew that fear of the uninvited guests in human lives—of sudden death and disease and disability—

manifested most concretely in the world through the seeking out of insurance products. The insurance agents knew how to harness and to direct these tenuous fears into the very tangible action that is the purchase of insurance products; it was practically in their job description to do so.

And The Guest was right there with them, beside every pitch, every skilful insinuation, every matter-of-fact promise of *prudence* and *peace of mind*, every signature on a new insurance policy.

Harnessing the worldly and palpable translation of fear to will to action, The Guest quickly amassed battalions of smoke demons: each one immensely powerful, engorged with the strength of human terror, and ready for deployment.

It was time to make his declaration of war.

~*~

Leonard stared at the television screen in confusion. He was back in the dingy two-room apartment he shared with his mother. The newly minted recruits were given a week's worth of block leave before embarking on their assigned vocations. Leonard was, to nobody's surprise, one of the handful from his cohort selected to attend the Officer Cadet School, where he would train for nine months before commissioning as a second lieutenant of the Singapore Armed Forces.

However, that was the furthest thing from his mind as he watched the horrific scene unfold on the news with all the incongruity of a very bad dream.

It was an aerial video of Parliament House, its angular stateliness and prominent national crest immediately recognisable. Right before the iconic architecture were its symmetrical green lawns, sprawling and stretching ahead of the main building like open arms. The Marina Bay Sands luxury hotel peeked out the back, as if stamping the scene with an incontrovertible Singaporeanness that it did for countless tourist trinkets.

On the two green lawns were...

Leonard blinked his eyes hard and scrutinised the screen, unsure if he was actually seeing what he saw. It looked like a scene from a horror movie, its striking effect undiminished by the lack of special effects.

On the two green lawns were...

Six tall stakes plunged deep into the turf of each lawn.

Each stake, about twelve feet in height, bore a badly burned corpse. The remains of a man, or woman. Brutally skewered onto the thick wooden rod. From the rear, up the gut, through to the oesophagus, and out.

Leonard swallowed intensely, fighting the bile that threatened to free itself abruptly from the confines of his body.

Six stakes bearing six burned bodies on each grass lawn.

Twelve in total for two grass lawns.

That was not all. As the drone camera tightened the shot, Leonard could see more bodies arrayed directly in front of the grotesque skewers.

Equally charred bodies, arranged, in a maniacal parody

of camp games or graduation photography, to form a word that can be read from height.

THANK YOU.

A single word on each lawn.

THANK.

YOU.

Leonard felt his stomach then truly roiling in protest. His eyes watered from not blinking as he watched the footage in transfixed revulsion. These were human beings. These were people. These were most probably his countrymen. Skewered indifferently like meat to be eaten.

As if taunting the viewer, there was more. The camera shot tightened again, zooming in to a specific feature shared by all the burned corpses. Their hearts had been ripped out of their chests—the blackened organs now hung limply against the stark ribs. The edges of the wounds, or what could be seen of them, were ragged and uneven.

Shaking off his dazed reverie, he reached for his smartphone hurriedly, looking up the matter on the internet, praying it was some horrible joke; a hacker had gotten to the broadcast station; it was fake news, only fake news.

He scrolled through the top hits in the search engine, dread intensifying. *The Straits Times. Channel News Asia. Asia One. BBC News. CNN.*

Could a hacker have gotten to all the major news outlets? Could the major news outlets be reproducing faux footage without first checking the scene? It seemed most unlikely.

But it could not be real. Things like this did not happen in Singapore. Never did, never should. Could it?

A terrorist attack? Satanic cult? Film set? Advertising stunt?

Leonard could not imagine it being the work of an individual, for the wooden poles were extremely long—more than twice the height of an average person—and extremely wide in diameter. And if so, how did they ever manage to achieve this large-scale macabre installation without once attracting the attention of the security guards of Parliament House? Or passersby? Or anyone? It was inexplicable.

His phone began vibrating incessantly as text messages from various social media apps began pouring in, all feverishly discussing the incident; most of them incredulous and sceptical.

Who was the message intended for? What did it mean? Who was responsible? What was responsible?

Leonard shuddered and wished once again that Marie Rose were there beside him.

~*~

Days passed and nobody claimed responsibility for the grotesque installation at Parliament House. More mysteriously still, the extent of the damage to the charred corpses made it insurmountably challenging for police identification of the bodies and hence resulted in a complete dearth of leads to the perpetrator. On the wooden stakes, the police found no trace of fingerprints, hair, flakes of skin, or any identifiable bits of physical remainders. The news channels and social media platforms churned with fearful speculation and conspiracy theories of every shape, size and form. Nothing and no one was spared from suspicion. The citizens waited with bated breath for the perpetrator to make his next move. The government stepped up its defence and security measures.

The security guards on duty at Parliament House were arrested and questioned relentlessly. Key personnel were detained, more secretively, and questioned relentlessly.

Soon after, extremist groups began to make insidious and incendiary comments, opening up racial and religious fault lines. Commentators from all around the world plunged elbows-deep into the torrid speculation, with scores of "subject matter experts" chiming in and offering counsel. In a matter of days, the country was ruled by fear and suspicion. Neighbour suspected neighbour. Every family kept to itself and holed up in their apartments. Schools were closed for a time. Companies permitted their employees to telecommute as much as was possible.

Panic-buying at supermarkets ensued as many families attempted to stock up on non-perishable food products. Retailers offloaded their stocks at a record rate and frantically tried to re-supply as fast as the demand grew. The police were set to city patrol to prevent looting and misdemeanour.

Fortunately, the perceived threat remained much too nebulous at this point to spark any sort of grave incidents of public disorder. Nevertheless, orderly snaking queues began forming outside of obscure wholesale storehouses and supply depots as people turned away from emptying retail stores and gravitated towards any and every source of available foodstuff. People did what they could, as much as they could, and nothing more. The queues promptly dispersed by nightfall daily. No one wanted to be out in the dark.

The Prime Minister made the requisite reassurances to the people that investigations were ongoing and warned sharply against needless speculation. Unbeknownst to the public, the Prime Minister and his cabinet quietly squirrelled away into their heavily guarded respective safe houses. The Ministry of Defence and the Ministry of Home Affairs made their plans for the worst.

Perhaps it's a one-off stunt, some people commented hopefully, pleadingly. *Perhaps we are all over-reacting.*

Most others were not as optimistic. Online, the features of the installation were scrutinised, dissected, heatedly discussed, intellectualised, and scoured for symbolisation and hidden meanings.

What did it really mean? What is to come?

"It's a declaration of war by The Guest, and we have made no plans. We are too late," Lady Pontianak sighed heavily.

The Grassroots Committee of Ghosts and Monsters had convened an emergency War Council. All members flocked to the meeting immediately, despite not possessing one inkling of what a War Council meant. None of them had ever experienced a paranormal war. In the past, ghosts and monsters had judiciously refrained from interfering or getting involved in human wars.

Nevertheless, war times were lean times for ghosts and monsters. The old spirits had the Japanese occupation of the 1940s foremost in their minds as they gathered swiftly in the familiar dilapidated housing estate that now served as their Central Command Headquarters.

"We still don't know what his army looks like, who is fighting for him, and how and where they will fight," the Woman in the Red Dress ventured uneasily. "The over-the-top warning is utterly in line with his flamboyant style, that's for sure, but it gives us no clues on what he will do next."

"Should we be preparing to flee to Malaysia for the time being, lay low until things blow over? This is not our fight. The Guest has no quarrel with us, only with the humans," Auntie Chin added tentatively.

"I believe it's time for us to settle this matter once and for all. We have to take a vote. And from then on, this War Council will take a stand and not back down from it," Lady Pontianak had gotten to her feet. She looked round the conference table and acknowledged each ghost and monster present.

"Ancient ones, we the old spirits of Singapore... let us put this matter now to vote. Do we stand and fight?

Or should we retreat and come back when all is done and dusted?" Lady Pontianak gestured to Uncle Bhuta. "Uncle Bhuta will now be passing this pail around. Write down "Fight" or "Flee" on the paper you have before you, fold it, and place it into the pail. You do not have to write your name. But before you make a decision, I implore you, look deep into your hearts. If we even have one, that is. Now *that* I don't know for certain." She smiled sardonically.

The small blue plastic pail duly made its round from member to member. Lady Pontianak had been the first to cast her vote. The mood was solemn as the ghost and monsters scribbled their decisions on scraps of paper, folded them dutifully, and placed them reverently into the pail.

Finally, the pail came back to the head of the table. Lady Pontianak murmured for Uncle Bhuta to proceed with the counting. He cleared a spot on the table in front of him and began.

Opening the first slip of paper he drew from the pail, he read it, and placed it face-down on the table. Second slip, unfolded, read, and added to the first. Third slip, unfolded, read, and added to the pile. Fourth slip, unfolded, read— Uncle Bhuta paused—and placed it face-down far apart from the first pile. The second pile had begun.

And on he went, carefully sorting the slips of paper into two neat, distinct heaps on the table. Some moments passed, and the meeting members observed as one pile grew ostensibly larger than the other one. Uncle Bhuta kept up his even, steady pace, not slowing down or speeding up as the pile grew, heedless of the eyes of the meeting members fixed on his hands.

It was done. Uncle Bhuta showed the empty pail to the meeting and set it down.

Lady Pontianak spoke. "Now, we will reveal the results of the vote. We can see that the council has voted quite unanimously for one option over the other. We will be leaving these slips of paper, sorted as they are, untouched right here. You may check them later after the meeting if you wish."

Uncle Bhuta picked up one of the slips atop the larger pile. He held it up so the meeting members could see what was written on it.

FIGHT.

A collective murmur rippled across the conference table. It was decided. They would fight on the side of the humans, to defend them against The Guest and his army.

"Thank you for your vote. The War Council will honour it. But before that, I will say this as your old friend. If you had voted otherwise, you are free to leave after this meeting concludes. There will be no repercussions. No one will know what you have decided today, right at this moment. You will always be welcome back in Singapore after the war, if there is anything to come back to," Lady Pontianak announced.

"As for the rest of us, we will pour our energies into repelling The Guest and his army from this land. We will stand and fight for the humans, no matter the cost to our existence. We may not survive this. But for the sake of our humans and our land, we will act from this moment on as if we *will* be victorious. This is the only reality we *must* believe in now. We will defeat The Guest, his foot soldiers, and do everything we can to prevent them from setting foot in any part of Singapore ever again. Are you with me?"

"Yes, Ma'am!" the War Council roared in response.

"Alright." Lady Pontianak nodded. "Let's get to work."

As she sat down, the Child of the Bridge spoke. "It is bad that we are going in more or less blind. But we can rectify this. I will gather as much as covert intelligence on our enemy as I can, by hacking into government databases and assessing the information they have right now. It would be good too if we could all reach out to our networks of ghosts and monsters in our respective areas of haunting, to enlist their help. If not to fight, then as an ear to the ground to gather information."

The meeting members nodded their agreement.

"We do not know where The Guest will launch his first offensive, whether on the mainland, or via Singapore's small outlying islands. I will muster the ghosts and monsters of Pulau Tekong as well as those of the sister islands around us. Every spirit will count now," Marie Rose said.

"It is true that we do not know where the first attack will be. Or what form it will take. But we need to make our best guess, at the very least, and prepare a strategy for that eventuality. We cannot be sitting ducks, simply waiting to respond," the Eurasian vampire added.

"I agree with you. The Guest had mentioned that he

was child to the fears of modern society," Lady Pontianak picked up the relevant minutes of meeting that Uncle Bhuta had prepared. "And I quote: 'I am strong from the fear of uninvited guests in the lives of the people—terminal illness, existential anxiety, mental disorder, loneliness, humiliation, impotence, inadequacy, unfulfilled potential. I am strong from the fear of inequality—that those who have more should wield great power over the lives of those who have less.'"

"Thank goodness you captured him verbatim; he certainly is quite long-winded." The Chinese vampire smiled appreciatively at Uncle Bhuta, who smiled back.

"Let's walk in his shoes for a second. That pompous, self-important prick," the elder Marbles Child mused aloud. "So I have a large army of scary monsters now. Where would I attack first, in my quest to eventually enslave all humans of Singapore? Where am I strongest? Where would my power be concentrated?"

Picking up on his strand of thought immediately, the younger Marbles Child answered. "The most vulnerable segments of Singapore. The downtrodden, the needy, the poor. These humans would have the greatest cause to fear foreigners, strangers, and the unknown. Uninvited guests in their lives would hit them the hardest, as they do not have the financial capital to mitigate them well. And... *they are* the victims of inequality."

"Yes, that is good thinking," Lady Pontianak continued. "The Guest and his army would be strongest where fear of them is strongest. It would make sense for them to launch an attack in these very segments of Singapore, and not immediately in the bastions of human power and authority. They would need a good initial momentum and early victory to create maximum impact, and to encourage even more fear, which would then spread like wildfire and further feed their strength. I am thinking... old housing estates, rental flats, one or two-room flats. Where the vulnerable of Singapore reside."

The meeting members understood intimately the strength of the bonds to a spirit's birth place. The closer to its core, the more power the spirit possesses, to control and manipulate the fabric of reality. It was the same for all of them.

"We need to stop The Guest before he can establish a beachhead," said the Child of the Bridge. "We should raise defence forces at these vulnerable places where The Guest is likely to launch his first offense."

"Yes, I agree. The first act of the War Council will be to protect Singapore's places of vulnerability. Residential ghosts and monsters, you know these areas best." Lady Pontianak's voice was clear as a bell. "I shall hereby establish the Northern, Southern, Eastern, and Western Command, each corresponding to the locations in Singapore we need to protect first. I will name a Head Commander for each of these four defence forces. Your responsibility will be to muster and deploy all ghosts and monsters in your area to defend the residential estates of the vulnerable. As for you, Marie Rose, you will be the Head Commander of the

Auxiliary Force, consisting of ghosts and monsters of Pulau Tekong and its sister islands. The task of the Auxiliary Force shall be to provide reinforcements to areas that require it most when the fighting begins. Does everyone understand their responsibilities?"

"Yes, Ma'am!" answered the War Council.

"Good. If there are no objections, I hereby name myself the Chief of this War Council. From now on, we will re-convene here every twenty-four hours for updates on the situation, until further notice," Lady Pontianak concluded.

The ghosts and monsters banged their fists on the table to demonstrate their acquiescence.

"Right, let's win this war then," Lady Pontianak said, the hint of a smile playing around her lips.

The meeting members erupted into a din of indistinct battle cries.

It happened within the Northern Command.

Leonard saw it first, looking out the window as he set a kettle to boil, in preparation of dinner for his mother and himself. On the basketball court flanked by several old apartment blocks akin to his own, three or four smoke demons streamed out of the elongated shadows cast by a lowering sun. Despite their almost fluid-like shape, the demons scuttled along uncertainly on the hard court, their diamond eyes darting from side to side.

To his abject horror, Leonard saw that the basketball court was not empty. Two young boys, about ten or eleven years old, were playing at the other end of the basketball court from the smoke demons. An old man, presumably their grandfather, sat on the bench at the side lines.

Leonard squinted hard at the rollicking shapes of dark smoke tumbling towards the humans.

Excepting his grandmother and Marie Rose, it was the first time he had actually seen anything so ostentatiously supernatural. *Are they dangerous?* None of the ghosts he had interacted with were dangerous, per se. They could be scary, but…

Screams.

The smoke demons had reached their targets. As if frozen in a dreamscape, Leonard watched in astonishment as the monsters launched themselves bodily at the young boys. The boys could *see* them, in the way he could. And within seconds, the smoke demons had devised sharp claws from their vague tendrils and… ripped the hearts out from the boys' chests.

Feeling like a cartoon character, Leonard actually rubbed his eyes with his fists, disbelieving. He blinked hard. And looked again. The scene was unchanged, hideous in its stark cruelty. He watched, frozen, as the boys fell to the ground, red pulsating organs hanging bizarrely outside their ravaged flesh. Their faces bore identical expressions of utter astonishment as they gurgled and choked. Blood spewed from their mouths. Their limbs were twitching spasmodically. One of them had a hand hovering around his still-beating heart, uncertain and undecided, as if contemplating whether to thrust the torn organ crudely back into the body.

The smoke demons abandoned the convulsing bodies and reached for the old man, who was gaping in horror and unmoving from shock.

Leonard got over himself and sprang into action. Barely thinking, he seized two of the longest, sharpest knives they had in the kitchen and barrelled out of his home. He ran down the two flights of stairs from his apartment and dashed to the basketball court.

The smoke demons were clutching the old man's now lifeless body, its vital organ now too hanging monstrously outside its chest cavity.

For a moment, Leonard was unsure of himself. *I had hardly stopped to think. Just what am I planning to do?*

But then the demons moved, and he charged at them like a maniac.

As he got closer, he realised that he could barely discern the anatomy of the smoke demons. *Where was its head?* Their glinting diamond eyes circled freely around the amorphous shapes that made up the smoke demons' form, pointing now towards Leonard with gleeful malicious intent. *Where do I strike?*

Yelling incoherently, Leonard swung one of his knives and made a slashing motion as if to cut the nearest smoke demon into half.

And so he did. The smoke demon was sliced into two

halves, one gleaming eye on each. The halves quivered in the air for a heartbeat, as if uncertain for a moment.

And then, most gleefully, they joined back together again.

Seamlessly, flawlessly, the smoke demon was once again whole.

Before Leonard could process his shock, he felt the ground rumble right beneath his feet. A deafening roar sounded from behind him as the wind rose and he *felt* rather than saw the presence of a horde charging right at his back.

Without waiting for him to turn around, the old ghosts and monsters of the Northern Command leaped, wafted, whizzed, or flew—each employing their own preferred means of locomotion—toward the smoke demons. Leaving Leonard stunned in their wake, they fell upon the handfuls of evil, and using the weight of their years, their entire strength, their ancient powers, somehow, *squashed* the smoke demons out of existence.

Leonard could barely see what was happening as he watched the motley crew of spirits—deathly pale women with feet-length hair in white dresses, Chinese-styled vampires, European-styled vampires, amorphous great big monsters, animal-human chimeras, clackety skeletons, squat fat gremlins, vague humanish silhouettes upon which bore fatal-looking wounds, and many others—all piled onto the smoke demons, shrieking, bellowing, and cursing. Blinding rays of white light burst forth from beneath the rush of bodies as the last of the smoke demons exploded into oblivion.

"Did you make that light?"

"No, it wasn't me, was it you?"

The heap of assorted ghosts and monsters all started talking at once, looking around at each other in befuddlement.

"Wait, you know, I'm still not exactly sure how we killed them…"

"Yes, when I saw them, my first thought was to simply advance… I didn't really spare a thought as to what I was actually going to *do*…"

"What do you think did it? How *did* we kill them?"

"Guys, this was just a piteous handful. I think it was only the reconnaissance team…"

Leonard blinked, still holding his two kitchen knives in a death grip. He had gone pale. Numbly, he watched as the old ghosts and monsters righted themselves and almost comically adjusted their respective clothing and accoutrements. *Is this a nightmare? Am I going to wake up on my mattress any moment now, shell-shocked but relieved? Right now? How about now?*

Someone was screaming.

He turned and saw that masses of residents had gathered all along the common corridors and lift lobbies of the housing blocks surrounding the basketball court. Many were pointing, right past him, at the bewildering huddle of ghosts and monsters.

A few of the human-shaped ghosts threw up sardonic two-fingered salutes. The ghosts and monsters wanted the humans to be able to see them. They wanted the humans to know who were fighting for them.

"There was light," he heard himself saying. The ghosts and monsters turned to look at him. "The light some of you gave off dispelled the… creatures."

"Light banishing shadows… makes as much sense as any other logic, I suppose," said the Woman in the Red Dress. Her outlines were slightly blurry. She was far away from her parks and nature reserves.

The Northern Head Commander, who looked like a decapitated man holding his chopped-off head under his arm like a bowling ball, started to speak, the lips on his disconnected head moving. "Guys, guys, just picture the very power you draw on in effecting your haunting sessions. It is the same source, the same channel. Now imagine turning it into the light that will banish the smoke demons. We twist the reins of reality as we are used to doing. This time, it's simply a slightly different way of manifesting in the world."

"I do use simple lighting effects when I conduct my hauntings. I suppose I can somehow concentrate this particular feature and… amplify it when they next come," said one of the long-haired female ghosts. A few others nodded in agreement.

"Geez, how do we get them to stop screaming?" one of the sprites said irritably, jabbing a finger at the increasing crowds of residents now gathered at the common areas.

Amidst the hullabaloo, night had fallen.

The wind was slightly cold against Leonard's legs, clad only in scant exercise shorts. He was barefoot and a short scratch on his heel was bleeding a little.

"Leonard! Leonard!" His mother was suddenly running towards him, her gaze wild as it flitted uncomprehendingly from her son to the bizarre fray. "What are you doing? Are you hurt?"

As he started towards his mother, something caught the corner of his eye.

"LOOK OUT!" he shouted to the old ghosts and monsters.

It was too late.

An entire battalion of almost five hundred smoke demons had begun pouring out of the shadows. The first row of inky soldiers had leapt onto several of the old ghosts and monsters and methodically ripped them to shreds.

Shreds.

The miniscule pieces of the humans' allies shimmered in the air for a glittering second, then promptly winked out of existence.

Leonard felt slightly dizzy. There was no time to wrap his head around what was happening. He ran from the battleground, almost colliding with his mother as he flung his arms around her awestruck body and started pulling her with him. They ran back towards their apartment block.

"Get back into your homes! Bolt the doors!" he yelled up to the residents huddled in shock, watching. He had no idea if what he said would make any difference, but he said it anyway. Doing something felt better than simply standing by and watching the carnage unfold on the basketball court.

There was a thunderous patter of feet and flinging of doors as the residents immediately complied. The screaming children were anxiously shushed. Danger had arrived and self-preservation was first and foremost.

The Northern Command valiantly stood their ground, trying to hold back the tidal forces of The Guest's army. The old ghosts and monsters produced piercing white light in any way they could. Beaming from outstretched palms, emanating from gaping mouths, streaking from unearthly eyes. The ancient ones fought as hard as they could to stop the smoke demons from reaching the humans in the residential blocks. The demons were fast and nimble, and oddly coordinated, like a swarm endowed with a hive mind.

Two of them broke through the line of defence and started bounding after the first humans in sight—Leonard and his mother, who were still running towards their block.

Leonard saw them. They were impossibly fast. There was no way they could both get back to their house without the smoke demons catching up with them.

"Run, Ma! Go back to the house!" he yelled as he stopped running and faced the oncoming demons. He readied his kitchen knives.

As the smoke demons reached him, he took a leaf from their book and started slashing at them wildly, endeavouring to slice them into as many pieces as possible. It felt to him as though he were truly hacking at the air with the knives: the blades parted whorls of thick smoke that seemed insubstantial. He did not dare stop his knives, wary not to permit them any opportunity to re-combine into single entities capable of clawing his heart out.

His all-too-mortal arms began to tire. His muscles screamed in protest.

"Help, someone!" Leonard bellowed, willing for a ghost or monster to come to his rescue for a second time.

Beyond his small struggle, the larger battle raged. The Northern Command was faltering. More and more smoke demons began to break through and started scampering towards the residential blocks.

His arms were on the verge of giving out completely.

Just then, a throng of unidentified beings advanced from the distant skies to the battlefield.

Leonard's heart skipped with hope as they neared. They were not dark smoke swirls. It was a ragtag battalion of assorted ghosts and monsters, their countenances horrifying and ugly, like the cast of a blockbuster horror extravaganza. They looked truly fearsome. They looked like hope.

"Here! Somebody, help, please!" he yelled again.

A small body was rushing in his direction at breakneck speed. He caught a glimpse of swirly skirt and silken blouse. It was Marie Rose. She was carrying a SAR 21 assault rifle and aiming it at the smoke demons besieging him.

Just as he opened his mouth to tell her that bullets would not work against them, she had reached his side and pushed her finger against the trigger. A shaft of the same piercing white light he had seen the old ghosts and monsters produce on the battlefield surged forth and obliterated the straggly pieces of the smoke demons that were still struggling to re-combine themselves.

"Thank you," Leonard panted, dropping his leaden arms to his sides. He did not let go of the knives.

"Don't go back to your house," Marie Rose said urgently, her eyes wild. "It's not safe there. If they break through, they will enter the apartments and kill you all. Go far away. Get away from these blocks."

She'd barely finished her last word when she turned away from Leonard and hurtled toward the battlefield. She moved as if a gust impelled her small thin back; her feet unmoving, her hands poised at the ready on her rifle. Leonard thought, absurdly, that if there were a word that denoted an immensely fast version of floating, only that would adequately describe the way she was moving. His heart constricted at the thought of her going toward, and not away from, the fierce battle that was raging between the old spirits and the new.

But there was no time to waste. He turned to the residential blocks and wondered how he could possibly get all of the residents to evacuate as quickly as possible.

"We have to leave now!" Leonard yelled as he reached the ground level of his apartment block. Some of the residents were milling about outside their homes, gaping at the scene.

"We have to leave! It's not safe to stay! Come on!" Leonard

continued, rapping on the doors of the several units on the ground floor. "Open up! We have to leave!"

He spent precious time going round the first and second floors, knocking on all the doors of the units. Unbeknownst to him, a small group of smoke demons had successfully breached the Northern Command lines and were scuttling up the stairs.

After completing the first and second floors (many had blatantly refused to open up), he sprinted towards the third floor, where his home was.

"Ma!" Leonard was shouting as he ran. "Ma, we have to leave right now! It's not safe to stay here!"

The breath seized in his throat as he rounded the corner and his apartment door came into view. A lone smoke demon was oozing *out* from beneath the door. It methodically headed for the next door down the row, swiftly squeezing into the crack beneath his neighbour's door and entering the house.

Choking back his fear, Leonard flung the door open and hurtled into his house. "Ma! Are you here?" he whispered as loudly as he could.

Silence reigned. The apartment looked deserted.

Leonard opened the door to the lone bedroom and there his mother was, lying supine on the mattress on the floor. She was unnervingly still. A hunk of her long hair had fallen across her face.

He stepped closer.

Her heart had been ripped out of her chest.

Leonard   felt   as   though   the   blood   was   drained

instantaneously from his entire body. His palms grew clammy and the two knives, so precious to him just moments before, slipped uselessly out of his grasp and clattered onto the floor. Despite the horrifying scene before him, a wave of fatigue washed oddly over him. He had never felt so exhausted in his life. He wanted to close his eyes and go to sleep for a thousand years.

He slid to the floor slowly, ashen. His knees were barely able to support his weight on the ground. His body grew leaden and the very thought of motion became unbearable. A fog descended on his mind, blocking out any thoughts of immediate danger and self-preservation.

His mother was so pale. The grotesque wound on her chest blossomed like a hothouse flower. The room was already beginning to smell.

Just then, Leonard vaguely heard the sound of the main door opening again. He could not bring himself to stand up, to pick up the knives, to turn around. He was so, so tired. His mother needed him there. The world could crumble around his knees right there and then and he would not move a limb. This was exactly where he needed to be.

Footsteps sounded as something or someone very quickly closed the short distance from the main door to the bedroom.

"Leonard! Leonard!" he vaguely heard an urgent whisper. He was not sure; his ears felt muffled.

It was Marie Rose. He felt her small presence beside him. She had crept down to her knees as well. Her hands were on him.

"Leonard," she whispered again. Suddenly, her arms were around him. She cradled his head in her chest like one would comfort a crying toddler.

"We have to go," she said. "I'm so, so sorry, but we have to leave now. The Northern Command is on the retreat. This place will be overrun by the smoke demons soon. Let's go."

Leonard held on to her arm like a life raft. He tried to speak, but his tongue was glued to the roof of his mouth. His limbs refused to obey him.

"Come, Leonard…" Marie Rose was tugging at him now, trying to get him to move. "We have to go!"

Suddenly, her body stiffened as though his immobility had infected her. She was staring at his mother's body.

Leonard's mother had suddenly opened her eyes.

Opening them was an understatement; her eyes bulged so far out their sockets they fairly threatened to escape the confines of their constraining flesh. Stiffly, the corpse sat up on the mattress, a perfect ninety-degree right angle. And then she began to stand up, her motions jerky and inhuman. The heart that dangled from twists of gristle and muscle began swaying obscenely against her tattered chest.

Leonard could not help swelling with hope. *She's alive!*

"Ma!" he cried out. "Ma! I'm here… Ma…" He started to move forward, to reach out for his mother.

"No, Leonard!" Marie Rose wrenched him from the ground with a sudden burst of supernatural strength.

"Marie Rose… she's alive! We need to help her!" Leonard pleaded.

His mother's vacant, unseeing gaze had turned to them. Her mouth slowly opened, as if to speak, but it went on opening, and opening, and opening. It was a snarl. The sound was incomplete; it was abruptly seized as the corpse's lower jaw stretched too far away from the rest of its face and dislocated completely. It fell away and sagged onto the corpse's collar bones amidst a crimson tangle of torn flesh, tendons, and bone.

She started to stagger towards them, her hands outstretched in their direction like claws.

"LEONARD, RUN!" Marie Rose shrieked as they both reeled.

She gripped his arm and pulled him bodily from the room. She was not sure if she would be able to fly as she normally did, with the additional weight now in tow. But she tried.

And succeeded. Marie Rose and Leonard burst out of the apartment in ungodly haste as behind them, the reanimated corpse started gaining jerky speed, albeit with an outlandishly rigid gait. Its eyes were still glazed over with a milky, unseeing film.

Marie Rose held tight to Leonard's forearm and they sailed away into the night sky.

~*~

As soon as the deserted building that was the Central Command Headquarters came into sight, Marie Rose and

Leonard came tumbling down from the air onto a patch of grass. Marie Rose was getting pale, and alarmingly, her outlines had taken on a slightly blurry edge. She looked like she was beginning to fade.

Leonard gripped her chin firmly but gently in his hand. "Marie Rose, are you alright? You have to stay with me."

She lifted her eyes to gaze back into his, unblinking. "I'm fine, Leonard. It's been… a long night. I'm fine. I just need to rest for a while."

Leonard helped to ease her down onto the grass into a prone position. She rested her head face-down atop her forearms for a minute, gathering her strength. Leonard rubbed her back briskly, as though he were trying to stimulate warmth or blood circulation in her body. Though she needed neither, his gentle assiduity comforted her and brought her some much-needed courage and fortitude.

After fifteen minutes, she righted herself and sat up beside Leonard, resting her head lightly against his deltoid.

"I'm so sorry about your mother," she began. "I'm sorry that the old ghosts and monsters were not able to hold the line back there in your estate."

Leonard rubbed his temples with his knuckles. He had so many questions he did not know where to start. He did not understand anything.

"Who were they, back there? Why were they attacking us? How did they… *raise the dead*? Are the old ghosts and monsters helping us? Why?" the questions exploded from him in a torrential deluge.

Marie Rose sighed. "I don't know if I can answer your questions as well as you deserve. I can only try."

So she told him. She told him about The Guest who had gatecrashed the meeting of the Grassroots Committee of Ghosts and Monsters. About his indecent proposal. About the formation of the War Council and their decision to defend the humans. About their prediction of his first targets, which proved to be more or less accurate. About their gross underestimation of his forces. About the Northern Command tasked to defend his estate, and the Auxiliary Force that she led.

"The areas under the Northern, Southern, Eastern, and Western Command were all attacked at the same time tonight," Marie Rose explained. "The battlefront at the Northern Command was… the most intense. That was why the Auxiliary Force was deployed to fight there. But even then, we started to lose ground… and warriors… so quickly. And badly. We had to retreat. What remained of us… we fled and stood by as the smoke demons infiltrated the estate."

There were tears in her eyes. "What happened to your mother… It most probably happened to every human who had stayed behind in their homes. This we had no idea. That The Guest would be able to raise the dead. And most probably have them fight in his army now."

Her voice was shaking. Marie Rose willed herself to be strong. She was a warrior and a commander now. There were others counting on her. She could not crumble. She lifted her head high.

"What's going to happen now?" Leonard asked wearily. It had been a very, very strange night.

"The War Council will convene shortly. I'll need to be there to rally my troops. And await further commands from the Chief." Marie Rose realised now that Leonard could not go back to his home, where it was likely to be crawling with smoke demons. "Come with me. I need you."

Leonard nodded. "Whatever you require of me," he said, unable to keep a small smile from his voice. "…Ma'am."

8

THE THREE DAYS' WAR

The Head Commanders were reporting their casualties. It was a staggering number, considering that they had only just fought their first battles. The Northern Command and the Auxiliary Force had lost the most warriors. None of the defence forces were able to prevent The Guest's army from establishing his primary bases in the vulnerable estates. The old ghosts and monsters had lost the battle. Most disturbingly, none of them had anticipated The Guest's ability to reanimate the murdered humans and to absorb them into his army. The dead now fought for the enemy.

A sense of despair was palpable around the conference table. The bulk of the defence troops had stood down after the final roll call of the night. Only the original members of the Grassroots Committee of Ghosts and Monsters remained to re-convene the War Council. Morale was low. The commanders kept their heads lowered in shame. They had failed in their duty to protect the humans under their care.

Only Leonard could not help his eyes darting about the

conference table in great astonishment, gawking quite openly at the appearances the old ghosts and monsters adopted whilst off-duty. He could not believe Lady Pontianak could look like an elegant retired air stewardess, with her impeccable chignon and ramrod-straight posture. Uncle Bhuta was a distinguished elderly Indian gentleman clad in a resplendent brocade silk *sherwani* suit, topped off with the most magnificent salt-and-pepper beard. The Marbles Children were handsome youths of unknown age, dressed in popular brand-name polo tees and chino shorts. The Woman in the Red Dress, whom he had met earlier on the basketball court, was familiar to him; however she now allowed her long wavy tresses to cascade down her bare shoulders, grazing her small waist in the most alluring fashion.

Before he could finish scrutinising each of the meeting members, Leonard heard his name being uttered. Marie Rose was introducing him to the Chief of the War Council. She informed the meeting of his display of military valour on the battlefield despite possessing no supernatural abilities. The Head Commander, who had witnessed it all, concurred and complimented Leonard on his dexterity with the kitchen knives. "He tried to save the residents, putting their lives ahead of his own," Marie Rose highlighted to the Council.

Lady Pontianak nodded. Leonard wanted to add that the troops of the Northern Command were braver that night than he could ever be in a hundred lifetimes. That they and Marie Rose had saved his life more times than he could remember. That the humans of Singapore should forever be in debt to the old ghosts and monsters for their heartrending sacrifices. But the look on Lady Pontianak's face told him that she knew all of this, and more. The wisdom and years in her eyes were shining.

"We all did our best. Many of our friends and comrades died for the cause tonight. I know none of us were ever technically *alive*. In the way that humans are. But still. Those lost to us tonight will most likely never be able to come back again. We have lost this battle," Lady Pontianak said to her War Council. "But not the war. Not yet. We have to remember that."

The meeting members nodded in agreement. Their faces were solemn.

"The beachhead has been established," the Child of the Bridge said bitterly. "The Guest will now be able to re-group and consolidate his troops there, including the newly-enlisted army of the dead. And from these positions of strength, proceed to take on more and more. Until? What would constitute a victory to him?"

"His army can now grow at an exponential rate, as they go on to kill more humans and to add the undead to their ranks," Lady Pontianak deliberated. "His forces will then be strong enough to take on the very bastions of human power. The Ministries. Parliament House itself. Then, he will rule. As promised."

Each of the meeting members grimaced, including Leonard. It sounded so... inevitable.

"What can we do? What can... *I* do?" Leonard said

suddenly. He was overwhelmed by the fact that the old ghosts and monsters were fighting this war on behalf of the humans. Without them, the humans would be utterly helpless. Bullets and blades were useless against the preternatural army of smoke. Grenades, explosives, bombs? They were worth a try, but also most probably just as ineffective. The humans were sitting ducks, awaiting death, or worse.

"Surely the humans can do something. To help. To do some damage to The Guest and his army," Leonard continued. "The ancient ones can't continue alone. We need to stand together."

He could see the muted despair in their eyes. What *could* the humans do, besides dying haplessly and adding to the ranks of the enemy?

Leonard refused to be deterred. He forged on, thinking aloud. "If The Guest and his dark forces are sustained by the fear of the humans, could we do anything to weaken such sustenance? If the opposite of fear is courage, would demonstrating courage as a people united be able to change anything?"

Marie Rose thought then of his boldness, his utter dauntlessness, as he had waved his pathetic kitchen knives at his supernatural foe, dashing them into pieces and desperately thwarting their recombination.

"Yes, I agree with Leonard that man and spirit should work hand in hand," Marie Rose said. "If Leonard would be able to rally the support of brave men and women, they could fight alongside us. They could make the destruction of the smoke demons so much faster, if they broke them up into temporarily incapacitated pieces, with the use of any sort of improvised weapon, like Leonard did. The ghosts and monsters could then destroy them with a single blast of light. It would be quicker. And more effective. We could increase *our* ranks too."

"This would indeed require great courage. And in turn, the display of courage as the opposite of fear might even be helpful in diminishing the core strength of The Guest and his army," the Northern Head Commander added.

Lady Pontianak looked thoughtful. "I can only agree with these very sound tactics. It would be best if humans could be roped in to help with the war effort. Besides, what you just said goes beyond the matter of padding our ranks for the war. In the long term, for ultimate victory, the humans of Singapore would have to dismantle The Guest's source of sustenance. So you say the opposite of fear is courage. It can also be… solidarity. Trust. Security. Faith. Love."

Leonard looked grim as he tried for a moment to contemplate his countrymen's love for one another. It was tenuous at best. "Perhaps we should start with courage, first. One battle at a time. I don't know how I would be able to get my message to all the humans of Singapore out there fast. Perhaps social media would be a good starting point. I'm sure there is already a hashtag on Twitter out there for the… carnage that happened tonight."

He then shook his head wryly. "But I am now a homeless man. I will need a computer… stable internet connection…

recording equipment. It's time for me to make my first YouTube video."

"Say no more," said the Child of the Bridge, newly-minted professional hacker and computer specialist.

~*~

Leonard fidgeted. He felt slightly foolish as he sat on a crude plastic stool set against a blank wall, facing the camera that had been mounted on a tripod. It seemed to him that he was merely an insignificant imposter. What authority did he really have, to rally the humans of Singapore to fight in this paranormal war? He was not the Chief of Defence. He was not the Minister for Home Affairs. But he had something none of them did. The truth of the matter. The truth the people needed to know at once.

Bolstering his spirit, he composed himself and judiciously affected a calm, neutral expression. He was simply a messenger. Nothing more, nothing less.

"There is indeed a Twitter hashtag trending now. It's *#NightofSmokeandBlood*. People are sharing the videos and pictures they managed to capture of the battles. The mainstream media channels are on to it as well," the Child of the Bridge briefed him.

"Alright," Leonard said. "Let's do it. We have to lead this conversation, now."

The Child of the Bridge nodded and carefully set down his stolen smartphone. It was an expensive one. He fiddled with the settings on the camera and gave a thumbs up. All systems go. He pushed the Record button.

Leonard took a breath. There was so much to say.

He began. "Fellow humans of Singapore. My name is Leonard Liu. I am a Singaporean son. I have... what you probably all know as the 'third eye'; I can see ghosts and monsters. Not that it matters now. All of you can see them now. Some of you have seen them and come to survive them. I am one of the fortunate ones."

He paused, suddenly struck by the force of a thought of his mother. He let the pain pass. "I am making this video to tell you all I know about the Night of Smoke and Blood. Perhaps you have witnessed it yourself. Perhaps you have seen the pictures and videos circulating the internet. Perhaps you have... lost someone you loved this night. Evil has come to our land. Our country has been invaded. These invaders are not beings of flesh and blood as we are. They are born of old magic and new fears..."

Leonard spoke for close to twenty minutes without stopping. He kept his grief tightly restrained as he talked about the monstrous foe whose army had killed his mother and in turn transmuted her into a monster as well. About how The Guest came to be, and why he came to be. About the old ghosts and monsters, who had lived alongside the humans of Singapore from time immemorial, and who had now come to defend them and to fight for them. About how the smoke demons killed, how they could be killed, and how they couldn't be killed. About the war that had just begun, a war the old ghosts and monsters were already on the verge of losing. About the real source of The Guest's strength, and how he may be defeated.

"The ancient ghosts and monsters have sacrificed themselves for our war. The war for our soil, our sovereignty. I can say this for certain: the Night of Smoke and Blood will not be the last of it. The Guest means to rule us, to have us under yoke and chain. We need every able man and woman to stand beside the old ghosts and monsters and to join the fight. You know what you have to do. This will only succeed if we work together. We need to show The Guest and his army that we are not afraid. That we have no fear. There is nothing left for us now, but victory or death."

Drained, Leonard nodded at the Child of the Bridge. He turned the camera off.

"Well done," the Child of the Bridge said solemnly. "I will upload this immediately and make sure it reaches every corner of the World Wide Web." He could not keep his signature cheeky mischief from his voice.

Marie Rose stood at the door.

"Come, get some rest. We will need you with us when the fighting begins again."

She led Leonard to the conference room where the War Council was held. She had improvised a rough bed for him, a nest of blankets and pillows arranged neatly on the long table.

"I… er… *borrowed* them from the nearest hotel. From a vacant suite. I'll return them when this is all over, of course."

Leonard smiled. The duvet was thick and inviting, the pillows fluffy and high. It was a bed fit for a king.

"Thank you so much, Marie Rose. For everything," he said, climbing onto the table.

His head touched the pillows and he fell asleep in seconds.

~*~

The Guest hummed happily as he walked the ground, surveying his new military bases. His army was growing stronger. He had to spend some time organising the reanimated dead, who were not very bright, but fortunately possessing a good strong bloodlust just waiting to be channelled for more violence and murder. The Guest was powerful, and they could feel it. They flocked to him like moths to a candle. They were ready to do his bidding alongside his children of smoke and diamonds. The Guest was so pleased he could barely stop himself from bursting into joyous laughter. *So this was why villains laughed so maniacally in films and cartoons,* he thought to himself. *Power is happiness. Power is joy.* He had never felt so alive.

"I am certainly no cartoon villain," he announced to no one in particular. "Just you wait. I will give you more than you ever wanted in your wildest dreams. I am a conqueror, a forger of empires. You will be proud to call yourself my subject, because only I can give you power on earth like no other nation can and will ever possess. The next global superpower of the twenty-first century? That would be *Singapore.*"

He stopped holding back and released the riotous laughter that bubbled up within him, deep and diabolical in spite of its effervescence.

~*~

As expected, Leonard Liu's video spread like wildfire on the internet: retweets, links on Instagram and Facebook, forwarded messages on WhatsApp, Telegram. It was all the humans of Singapore could talk about the next day. A few survivors from Leonard's estate had come forward to corroborate his story. Some of them had videos of Leonard's scuffle with the smoke demons featuring his now iconic kitchen knives.

The humans of Singapore heeded his call. The next day, they unearthed all manner of sharp objects from every corner of their homes. Whetstones were dully exhumed from dusty dwelling places and gainfully utilised, in many households for the first time in years. The uninitiated onlooker could be forgiven for thinking that the nation was preparing for the biggest cook-out in the history of the world.

But the mood was grim. No one wanted to have their hearts ripped out their chests without first putting up a fight. Men and women alike jumped at shadows and startled at innocuous noises. The elderly and the superstitious laid out splendid offerings for the old ghosts and monsters, veritable feasts fit for emperors and sages. Mists of incense and joss sticks upon crimson altars eddied the homes of Singapore.

Thank you for defending us. Thank you for fighting for us.

~*~

The bright light of the day yielded to periwinkle clouds shielding the retiring sun. Long shadows unfurled; the silhouettes of trees and buildings and lampposts taking on ominous nuances. No one dared to venture the slightest hope that the night would pass uneventfully.

And they were right.

Smoke demons slithered forth from what seemed like every other pool of shadow in the country. Close on their heels were the lumbering dead, their motions an offensive parody of the living.

Without warning, battles erupted in the immediate vicinity of all four of The Guest's bases at once.

They were in homes. They were in the kopitiams, the community centres, the shopping malls, the MRT stations, the bus terminals, the parks and nature reserves, the heartlands.

The old ghosts and monsters were compelled to spread their defence forces thin, scrambling urgently to cover all ground. Leonard kept close to Marie Rose. The Northern Command concentrated their forces at and around the estate which The Guest had won during the Night of Smoke and Blood.

A significant number of the resurrected dead were still gathered at the housing estate where they were spawned, yet to be deployed to battle.

"Let's hope that the fire would destroy them! Or slow them, at the very least!" Leonard was yelling to be heard above the din.

A short distance from The Guest's northern base, men and women were screaming and bellowing as they slashed at the air frantically with all manner of sharp objects. The old ghosts and monsters were there beside them, blasting the resultant fragments into oblivion. They were working as methodically as they could, indeed reminiscent of the chaotic order presiding in a restaurant kitchen on a Friday evening—each did their part and passed it on.

Despite their valiant efforts, many humans increasingly fell prey to the fluctuating talons of the smoke demons. Before their corpses grew cold, they were up and blundering about unseeingly, laying waste to their fellow countrymen with leaden conviction.

Leonard and Marie Rose led a small team, hauling massive containers of liquid kerosene pilfered from industrial warehouses.

"It won't be easy to set the whole block on fire. It simply won't spread from house to house because of the fire-proof doors," Marie Rose said. "We have to lure the army of the dead out."

Leonard swallowed his fear.

He headed toward the foot of his apartment block. From the corner of his eye, he could see the fateful basketball court where he had watched the night before as two boys and their grandfather were slaughtered in cold blood.

He held a *parang* knife in each hand.

Breathe in slowly through your nose, breathe out even slower through your mouth.

He concentrated on the breaths inflating and deflating his stomach. There was a slight breeze rising. The air felt clean and clear. The neighbourhood was old and familiar around him, like a beloved, well-worn sweater.

He could almost picture himself as a schoolboy, running up the stairs two at a time, clutching coloured ices or animal-shaped biscuits. He remembered himself as a child, playing hide-and-seek with his mother on the open ground floor of their block. He had started crying when she hid herself for too long. She had then emerged with laughter in her eyes and taken him into her arms, cooing. *Silly boy, it is only a game.* He remembered when she used to cook for him, homely dishes that no restaurant could ever reproduce. He remembered the day his father did not return home. His mother had sat at the dining table from dusk to dawn, growing paler and more withdrawn with every hour.

The memories pained him. But they were now only colourful stories in his head. They were no longer real. He looked up the apartment block and picked out the familiar door of his former home.

"Ma!" Leonard shouted. His voice carried far. "Ma! It's Leonard! I'm here!"

He continued calling for his mother for several minutes. In that time, many doors had opened. The smell of rotting flesh filled the air. Shuffle of feet. Inarticulate moans. The dead had started walking.

Leonard did not wait to see if his mother actually showed up. He started running towards the basketball court. Despite his fear, his senses were heightened and acute. His head was clear and his hands on the knives steady. He could see Marie Rose and her team in the distance. They had already doused the basketball court with the liquid kerosene and were waiting with lighters in hand. Leonard could hear the scuffle of feet behind him increasing in speed. It sounded like a flock of pigeons taking flight. They were coming.

Finally, he reached the basketball court and ventured a look over his shoulder. He was never able to conjure in his wildest imaginations or scariest nightmares such a horrific horde of shambling cadavers now chasing him.

The corpses were utterly stiff, almost comically so, like ironing boards propped vertically. They moved nothing but their feet; their arms were clapped rigidly to their sides. Many of them were covered in ruptured blisters, which continually oozed rancid-smelling fluid as they moved. Their skin appeared loose against their bones, sagging and wrinkling and flapping in the wind. Foul liquids streamed down from many a nose and mouth. On closer inspection, the ground on which they trod soon became dotted with tiny wriggling yellow maggots. Flies followed the horde around faithfully.

Leonard fought back the urge to retch. The stench from the hundred or so recently deceased was overpowering.

"They have to come closer!" Marie Rose was yelling. "We can't let any of them get away!"

Some of the walking dead appeared to respond to her voice. They departed the group and lumbered toward her general direction. Leonard fought the urge to run to her. He had to keep the bigger group together.

As if herding cattle, he goaded the shuffling, putrid throng, carefully, *carefully*, onto the basketball court, onto the spilled kerosene.

"Now!" he yelled.

Marie Rose's team dropped the lights and lit the court up. Flames roared and grew in strength quickly, setting the corpses on fire. They seemed unaware of their state of combustion, continuing along their shambling path, determined to reach Leonard.

Horrified, he abandoned caution and started running towards the rest of the team. Marie Rose had cut down the stray corpses that had started towards her using her trusty SAR 21. The small squad sprinted together towards a nearby pavilion situated on slightly higher ground. There, they huddled into a tight pack and shot at the few fiery corpses that careened after them. Fortunately, the bulk of the other corpses caught fire quickly and lay twitching on the hard court uncomprehendingly, allowing the flames to consume them.

The soldiers watched the burning corpses for a minute before Marie Rose roused them and indicated the next battleground requiring their reinforcement.

~*~

Marie Rose led the squad from the Auxiliary Force to the nearby kopitiam. The food centre had descended into nightmarish chaos. It was less of a battle and more of hand-to-hand combat on a sheer individual level, as a trickle of old ghosts and monsters struggled to protect the remaining stall owners who had not managed to disperse along with the rest of their patrons. The smoke demons lunged menacingly at the humans, while the old ghosts and monsters threw themselves in front of the humans, bodily shielding them from the enemy. They were getting increasingly outnumbered.

Marie Rose and her troops poured into the kopitiam.

"Cluster those bastards up! We can't win, picking them off one by one!" she yelled to her team.

The newcomers made a commotion of arriving, drawing the attention of the smoke demons away from their beleaguered victims. The demons hissed and spat, their hard diamond eyes brilliant with battle lust. Slowly and surely, the auxiliary squad drew them out from the depths of individual food stalls and goaded them into combat out in the relative open.

The old ghosts and monsters weaved in and out, diving and spinning and parrying and feinting, carefully dodging the lethal claws of the demons. Shafts of bright white beam pierced the air in choppy bursts, looking for all the world like an expensive light show at an amusement park. Some smoke demons were caught in the beams and vapourised. Many of the nimble ones easily circumvented the deadly trajectories, moving fast enough to pitch themselves onto the light-bringers. They took advantage of the intense concentration required in producing demon-killing light and almost easily minced their distracted opponent up into confetti.

Leonard kept close to Marie Rose. They worked as a tight, efficient team. He hacked at the smoke demons with his knives; she promptly followed with the rapid annihilation of the scattered shards. His crucial first strikes enabled her to work faster and at greater scale. They developed a rhythm and flow. Slaying the smoke demons came easily to them. It was as a performer felt—striking that first chord on stage and feeling his mind, his sense of self, melting away, becoming one with his instrument. And so it was with Leonard and Marie Rose—he and his knives, and she with her assault rifle—striking up a flawless tango that was also an effective killing machine, sweeping across the battleground with unstoppable ferocity and blasting hundreds of smoke demons into oblivion.

The auxiliary squad managed to shepherd the smoke demons harassing the kopitiam into one big oblivious assemblage.

"Now!" Marie Rose shouted.

All at once, the old ghosts and monsters summoned the light. The captive gang of smoke demons disappeared into the white firework and did not arise again.

~*~

For two nights, the humans of Singapore stood shoulder to shoulder with the old ghosts and monsters, resisting The Guest and his unholy army. Many who had watched Leonard's video responded to his call to arms valiantly.

Indeed, at certain shining moments, things appeared as though they could be turned around. Humans and spirits locked in perfect tandem, producing graceful moments of stunning teamwork, much as what Leonard and Marie Rose had come to acquire. *Slash and beam. Slash and beam.* In a few places, the humans actually gained momentum and succeeded in pushing back the army of smoke and corpses. The dazzling unity and defiant courage on display created weak spots amongst the enemy forces.

Sadly, the humans died faster than they could win.

The forces of The Guest grew larger and larger with every slain human. Eventually, sheer numbers prevailed. There were simply too many a smoke demon, too many a slavering cadaver, for the humans and their allies to continually drive back. Fresh troops stepped in almost instantaneously to pick up any slack. The reanimation of the dead exacted a most heavy toll.

So they retreated.

The survivors ran from the enemies and hid as well as they could, awaiting dawn's purifying light. After merely three days of fighting, slightly more than half of all the humans in Singapore remained properly alive. The old ghosts and monsters suffered grave losses. Nothing would be the same again.

9

THE BLACK FLAG

The Guest sat astride a beautiful horse. It was extraordinarily dark from ear to hoof, its coat gleaming like ripples of expensive silk in the morning light. It had black jewels for eyes, alert and intelligent; its black mane fringed a muscular back, shimmering with every slight toss of the mare's head; its black tail was luscious and active, whisking urgently from side to side. The horse was more shadow than animal, a satiny silhouette against the green grass lawn.

The green grass lawn of Parliament House.

All around The Guest, his army of smoke and corpses loomed. Shadows covered the two symmetrical lawns almost in entirety. The day had dawned, but the dark enemy remained. They were triumphant. They flaunted their existence—their hold on the physical world—defiantly, proudly. No more lurking in the shadows, no more striking in the dead of the night, no more yielding to the harsh light of day.

We are victorious. We are conquerors. Here we are. Look at us.

With the slightest incline of his head, The Guest signalled his shadowy troops to advance. The monstrous mass streamed across the red brick roads, the square foyer, and the slate grey colonnades that welcomed guests to the Parliament House. The smoke demons crept into every orifice of the building: doors, windows, gaps, crevices. The reanimated corpses lumbered through the main entrance unheedingly, mowing down the security guards that hurried forth to stop them. They ripped down and shredded the proud red ribbon banners bearing the white crescent and five stars on the building's façade. Human occupants were swiftly killed and added to the undead horde.

The Singapore Parliament was in session, but it made not a whit of difference to the invaders. The smoke demons swept into the hallowed assembly chamber, descending upon the pew-like seats on which Ministers and Members of Parliament sat. Shots rang out as the Serjeant-at-Arms and security officers grappled desperately with their handguns, attempting to fulfil their duties to serve and protect. The Speaker of Parliament was ripped unceremoniously from his throne by a handful of squabbling smoke demons eager for glory. Screams echoed down the hall, but not for long. The Guest's soldiers made quick work of the humans and promptly recruited them into their ranks.

There was high-pitched shattering all at once as the newly-minted undead stumbled clumsily into the glass balustrades of the raised Press Gallery overlooking the main assembly hall. Bodies fell from height everywhere and wrecked the handsome oak furniture.

The Guest cantered calmly into the assembly chamber atop his steed. He was clad in a sleekly tailored tuxedo, complete with matching black bow tie and a neat white pocket square. He had chosen to forgo his usual top hat that day, and his wavy close-cropped hair shone with a beatific gleam. With his dark eyes, aquiline nose, and straight white teeth, he looked every part the charismatic politician poised to shake hands and croon silky promises at a United Nations General Assembly meeting.

Sliding down his horse with practiced grace, he nonchalantly righted the toppled chair of the Speaker of Parliament beneath the bronze state crest. He had picked up the golden Mace of Parliament, swinging it around appreciatively. It was a beautiful object: the mace head comprised of an intricate winged lion caught mid-growl, clutching a trident, while the shaft bore the crest of the British Crown and the state crest, and was embossed with alternating lion heads and Chinese junk ships all the way down. He decided to keep it as a symbol of his newly earned authority.

He sank into the freshly vacated chair of the Speaker of Parliament, enjoying the view from the exalted vantage point. The chaos was still ongoing, albeit dwindling slightly, as more and more humans were slain. He could vaguely hear the sirens of what were most probably police vehicles, ambulances, and fire engines trilling outside the building.

He paid no heed. His foot soldiers would give them the warm welcome they needed.

After a few moments, The Guest grew bored of his meagre throne and swung up once more on his elegant dark horse. The chamber was emptying of humans. He nodded in the direction of the few remaining media personnel whose lives he had ordered his troops to spare. They cowered around their intricate cameras and recording equipment, furtively documenting the proceedings. The Guest hoped they had captured his most flattering angles.

With a small nudge of his heel, The Guest and his horse strolled from the chamber back toward the sunlight. He wanted to catch the best part.

"You might want to come along for this!" he called to the media personnel with a casual backward toss of his head. "It's going to be my favourite part."

Beneath the sure guidance of his rider, the horse trotted out of the chamber block, back to the spot between the twin rows of neatly manicured palm trees. The horse tossed its mane flippantly, scoffing at the sight of tropical wildness wrestled into regimental submission and ornamentation.

Rider and horse turned to face the Parliament House.

There were smoke demons scampering atop the ochre roof tiles. They hopped steadily up the jutting features of the building façade, heading for the highest point, where the national flag of Singapore flew from a lone flagstaff atop a triangular pinnacle. The comrades that followed carried a replacement flag—a rectangle piece of black cloth with nothing else on it.

In a few moments, the red-and-white flag of Singapore was irreverently stripped, its stars and crescent trampled carelessly underfoot. Up went the ominous black flag.

The wind had the audacity to breathe at that moment, sweeping the black flag up into a glorious flutter. All around the island, flags of Singapore were simultaneously torn down from each government building and replaced immediately by the black flags.

The deed was done. The Guest was ruler of the land.

The Guest cast a leisurely glance at the small group of media personnel huddling around their cameras. They had captured the scene of the black flag being hoisted.

"I'm available to give a media sound bite," he said almost politely. "Would you lot be interested?"

The small group looked at each other. They were pale and frightened. One of them started to nod.

"Good," The Guest said silkily and swept himself in front of the cameras. "Make sure you get that flag in the shot."

He looked straight into the cameras and started speaking.

"Humans of Singapore." He smiled, showing off the small white teeth that had a hint of shark about them.

"A very good day to you. My name is The Guest. You could call me... Xeno. It means pretty much the same thing.

"You who are watching this… Well. You sure have had a harrowing couple of days. I am so sorry for the extremely bad behaviour of my… friends." He leered, sweeping a hand toward a cluster of smoke demons loitering malevolently in the distant background.

"They have certainly been very rude. I have been away, travelling, and they simply… ran amok! How awful! I am aghast that you had to go through all that unpleasantness. It's a travesty, really." Xeno clicked his tongue sympathetically.

"Now that I'm back from my travels, have no fear. I have everything completely under control. I will protect all of you now. The army of smoke and corpses answer to me and me alone. And as you can see, we have, ah, taken the reins at every major organ of state. I am the rightful ruler of this land now," Xeno said delicately, almost apologetically, bringing his slim white fingers together.

"But you have absolutely nothing to worry about. Nothing! In fact, things can only go up from here. You will be happier than you have ever been under that miserable government of yours. All I ask of you is to trust me. Have faith in me. I will create a paradise here on earth, for both man and spirit. There will be no greater nation, no stronger superpower in this world than *Singapore*," Xeno said. In his hand was the Mace of Parliament stolen from the assembly chamber; he twirled it idly with his fingers. He liked the look of it. It completed his outfit.

"If you could forgive my grandiosity, I rather fancy myself

as… the Great Equaliser. Xeno the Great Equaliser. Under my benign dictatorship… yes, there's no point playing games here… as a most benevolent dictator, I will eradicate the struggle and suffering that plagued you in your previous lives. Forget the sorrows of the past! Today is glorious, and tomorrow, we will rule the world."

Leaning closer to the camera, Xeno dropped his voice. "But… do be careful. Should you slip up, well, I can't promise that I won't, too…"

He motioned at his smoke demons with the golden mace.

They leapt onto two of the media personnel who were not actively manning the cameras, and dragged them into the shot. On camera, the demons unhurriedly shaped their smoky tendrils into the signature sharp claws now painfully familiar to humans. They then proceeded to thrust them deep into their prisoners' chests. The captives screamed like all the humans did, as their beating hearts were torn out, right there and then. The tenacious organs remained pulsating on their own outside of their owners' ravaged chests for a full four minutes. One of the media personnel handling the camera fainted. The remaining other shakily turned the recording off.

"Well done, gentlemen. Hurry along to your editors now," Xeno said smoothly. "I have *so much* work to do." He turned and headed back into Parliament House.

~*~

Leonard had survived the Three Days' War.

Although the smoke demons and the reanimated dead had since traded their military bases for the state buildings, he could not bring himself to return to the house where his mother had been so brutally mutilated.

He returned instead to the deserted building that had hosted the War Council. He passed countless eerily empty flats, their doors and windows flung open, as though still expecting their owners to return at any moment.

Muttering an unnecessary apology, Leonard picked several vacant houses at random to hunt for provisions. A change of clean clothes. Some food and water. Cleaning and bathing supplies. Although he knew that their owners would not return, he felt immense guilt from blatantly helping himself to the items he needed. There was a grave-like stillness in the air. He barely saw any other humans on the streets. He wondered how many of them were left.

Back at the conference room, the hotel duvets and pillows still awaited him. He slumped into one of the chairs, weary to the bone. Some of the old ghosts and monsters were there. Lady Pontianak acknowledged him with a wan nod. She was not seated at her usual place, but at a corner of the room, her closed fists resting lightly on a small table. Her hair was unbound and unusually unkempt. Leonard caught a glimpse of the archetypical vengeful female ghost in the old wives' tales.

Marie Rose was there.

The old ghosts and monsters did not look well. They

were extremely faded in countenance and appeared listless and lethargic. Many stared into space insensibly. At times, they began to look like merely a trick of the eye—chance silhouettes arisen by the play of light and dust. Leonard had to look very hard to keep them from blending into the surroundings.

He was worried about Marie Rose. She had turned extremely pale and fairly translucent. She looked like a prototypical ghost in a ghost story. He was startled that he could see right through her.

He stood up from the chair abruptly and crossed the room. On his haunches beside her, he clasped both her hands in his, hard.

"Marie Rose," he whispered to her. "Stay with me. I am here. I see you. I remember you."

She looked at him, crestfallen.

"We lost the war," she whispered back. "What's going to happen now? We lost the war…"

She trembled violently all over. She was too distraught to cry. She felt all dried up inside, with nothing more to give.

"I failed my team. I lost so many of them… I am no *commander*," Marie Rose said bitterly. "I was just a stupid little girl, playing at war games. They followed me, and I led them to their deaths."

"*Don't say that*," Leonard growled angrily. He took hold of Marie Rose's shoulders and gave her a firm shake. "Stop it. Stop beating yourself up. We've all had enough of a beating, surely. I fought *beside you*. You are the bravest, most courageous girl I have met. You are *my* commander too, and I respect the hell out of you. You stood up to lead when you could have cowered and fled. You spoke when others were silent. You probably killed more than a thousand demons in three days, for heavens' sake! Just... what are you talking about?"

"Not enough," Marie Rose said flatly. "It wasn't enough. We were supposed to protect our humans, and we failed, again and again and again."

Leonard fell silent. He was so exhausted.

"Marie Rose, we did all that we could. Right now, we are all extremely tired and in no good shape to reflect and think and plan. We need rest. And then, we will get up and continue fighting. The war may be over, but the fight is not. We have to topple Xeno's reign," Leonard said, kneading her hands, stroking her hair, urging her vibrancy to return. "Don't give up, not yet..."

Marie Rose looked round the conference room. She looked at her old friends, fading and fraying at the edges. Even she found it hard to see them now. They were melting into the world.

Finally, tears gathered in her eyes.

"I'm sorry, Leonard," she said, her shoulders shaking. "I'm sorry, for all that you lost. I'm sorry for failing the humans of Singapore. I'm sorry we couldn't do better."

Leonard could not stop himself.

He closed the distance between them and kissed her. She was so warm in his arms, like a shaft of sun beam, like hot coffee on a rainy day, like a gentle breeze in evening light. She kissed him back fiercely, her tears running down into their lips. She was still shivering. Her silhouette was getting fainter and fainter. She felt herself slipping, slipping from the concreteness of the physical world.

"I'm falling…" she whispered against his lips. "I'm sorry, Leonard… I can't hold on…"

Leonard opened his eyes. Her hands in his were disappearing from view. The rest of her slowly followed, dimming and growing colourless. The objects behind her looked as though they were the ones gaining clarity, solidity, and vibrancy in colour. They were piercing through her. Less and less a girl and more and more the slanting rays of the soft afternoon sun, Marie Rose faded away.

"NO! No, wait! Marie Rose, wait!" Leonard grasped futilely at where her hands had been, as if trying to pull her back into reality. "No, no, no, no, no… Marie Rose!"

She was gone. There was nothing left where she had been, nestled against his chest. He looked round the room. The remaining old ghosts and monsters who were just there minutes ago had disappeared as well.

Leonard was alone in the room.

"No!" Leonard had started weeping too. "No! Come back… we still need you! Ancient ones, old ghosts and monsters of Singapore… please…! Please come back! I'm still here! I see you, and I need you! We still have to remove Xeno from power! Please! Please…"

He was sobbing violently. The room was so quiet.

"Lady Pontianak! Chairwoman of the Grassroots Committee of Ghosts and Monsters! Chief of the War Council! Please... we humans, *your humans*, still need you and your team... the fight is not over... please come back..."

Leonard called the names of the ghosts and monsters he had come to know, over and over and over again.

Marie Rose.
Lady Pontianak.
Uncle Bhuta.
The Marbles Children.
The Woman in the Red Dress.
The Child of the Bridge.
The Northern Commander.
Marie Rose.
Marie Rose.
Marie Rose.

He cried bitterly into his hands. He was bawling like a child lost in a shopping mall. He had not a shred of dignity or pride left in his bones. He wanted help. He wanted his mother. He wanted *Marie Rose*.

The pain that shredded through him left him doubled over. A sharp pain in his chest. A real pain.

He did not understand. Marie Rose had just been right there beside him. She had just been talking to him. Just like any other day; like in Pulau Tekong when she had laughed with him, curled up at the foot of his bunk bed, recounting funny moments of the day they had just shared; when she had guided him through his panic attack with that firm, unwavering voice of hers; when she had yelled at him so ferociously for slicing his hand open in that haunted old primary school; when, on the battlefield, she had issued short sharp commands and charged fearlessly at their enemies, rifle in hand. The memories riddled him like bullets. He could barely breathe from sobbing so hard.

Are you a man, or are you a child? he thought. *What would Marie Rose say if she saw you acting like such a pathetic wretch?*

He *wanted* her to yell at him. He wanted her to beat at him with her little fists. He wanted her to shove him hard and call him an idiot. He wanted her laughter. He wanted her tears. He wanted anything, *anything*, but this dreadful emptiness, this nothingness, this silence.

"Where are you? Where have you gone?" he said to the empty corners. "You *will* come back, won't you? Just like you did when I came looking for you in Pulau Tekong. I will look for you to the ends of this earth if I have to."

The room did not answer.

~*~

The humans of Singapore grieved for the loss of the old ghosts and monsters as much as they did their slain compatriots. Theories for the reason of their disappearance swirled the internet. Many of them came to the same consensus. They faded away, because they had become *beloved*. In fighting for the humans, in defending the humans, they had singlehandedly erased any fear the humans bore of them—the very fear that was the reason for their existence. And so they were gone. Like any human deprived of oxygen, water, food… they ceased to exist.

This tragedy was a double whammy for the humans, who now had to continue life as Xeno's subjects. They lost their defenders, and they knelt for a dictator. Many tried to revive the old ghosts and monsters by desperately laying out sumptuous offerings. They burnt enough joss sticks to pollute their living space. They reminisced about the old ghost stories they used to tell. But it was all in vain. The undercurrent of love flowed through their every act. The tragedy that was love had absolutely no effect in bringing the old ghosts and monsters back into existence.

Leonard tried to tell himself that he had always expected this day to come—the day when Marie Rose was gone from his life for good. He was a mortal, and she was a ghost. He suppose he had always known, right from the beginning, that they would never have any future worth speaking of together. Nevertheless, the loss struck him much harder than he could ever have imagined. He lived with it every day; the pain in his chest had become chronic, recurring at all times of day when something reminded him of Marie Rose. The familiar tightness in his muscles, that sudden sharp cramp… in a way, it became something he clung on to now. The pain meant that he remembered. It meant that he loved.

He did not dare to leave the dilapidated building that had served nobly as the Central Command Headquarters. He wanted to be there. *In case they came back.*

He reached out to his friends. Through the internet, the humans of Singapore grasped desperately for each other. *Where are you staying now? Come here, we have a group of us living together for better security. Come to this estate, there are quite a lot of us here. We have to stick together.*

The days and months that followed were jarring. While the nature of Xeno's battle strategy had meant that those who survived did so as an intact family unit according to their residences, the interconnectedness of the small island meant that everyone knew someone who had been slaughtered in the Three Days' War. Yet there could be no funerals, no memorials, no comforting last rites. The loss was incomprehensible, surreal. And most of all, before grief, there was fear—the acute fear that the dead would come back for those who were still alive. People had frequent nightmares featuring the transformation of their slain family and friends into that awful, distorted mockery of life—slack-jawed, blank-eye, rigid shuffle and outstretched claws.

Moreover, the abrupt change in leadership and administration left the country reeling. They had no running water for three months and no electricity for six. Parents were afraid to send their children back to school. Teachers had no students to go back to school for. People streamed into their former workplaces, only to find them half-empty and crippled. Foreign-owned companies had hastily shut down their satellite branches in Singapore. Masses of people found themselves unemployed overnight. That was, in fact, the least of their problems, for money itself became increasingly useless. People no longer knew the value of their currency. There were barely any shops open; those that did increasingly engaged in barter trade instead.

Xeno provided for the humans' basic needs. Stripped to its essentials, it was not logistically challenging to keep the human organism alive. There were food rationing stations, communal water sources (at which queues snaked everyday), and basic supply depots distributing the small miscellaneous provisions that made life bearable. The whole of Singapore resembled a refugee camp.

The only thing people no longer complained about was space. With half the population gone and foreigners long returned to their home countries, there was plenty of space left in Singapore. A single family could occupy an entire level of apartments if they wished. Curiously enough, nobody did so. The humans stuck even closer together. Every survivor desperately sought out news of remaining kin, friends, colleagues, acquaintances. They hungered for a familiar face more than any kind of material good. The first thing people did upon reuniting was to cry. They hugged and wept and clung to each other fiercely. It was a miracle to have survived the Three Days' War.

Leonard met up with the friends he had made at his basic military training course. They were historical relics of the life he last knew before the war. Training at Tekong felt like another lifetime, another person's memories. With the Ministry of Defence now defunct, they were no longer soldiers of the Singapore Armed Forces. But the very last event of their former life had been to celebrate their official proclamation as sworn defenders of the country.

Huddled in a small group over simple rationed food, they reminisced about the first day they met; the first day of their military training, where they had uttered the Singapore Armed Forces oath of allegiance, holding their palms open to the witnessing heavens:

We, members of the Singapore Armed Forces,
Do solemnly and sincerely pledge that
We will always bear true faith and allegiance
to the President and the Republic of Singapore.
We will always support and defend the Constitution.
We will preserve and protect
the honour and independence of our country
with our lives.

The group had started reciting the oath together merely jokingly at first, the punchline of some offhand jest. However, as their voices died down, secret unmanly tears came to the eyes of many.

We will preserve and protect
the honour and independence of our country
with our lives.

The lines bounced around their heads, stubbornly refusing to leave. As survivors of the Three Days' War, they were treasonous for allowing an invader to ravage their country, to spit upon the Constitution, and to transform the nation from republic to monarchy.

They had failed to uphold the oath they had solemnly sworn.

But it was not too late to make things right.

Oddly enough, for a time, life became easy, almost carefree. All of human concern was distilled to its most elemental and primordial—sheer brute survival. The calm that followed the carnage posed a sharp relief. An exhalation. *I lived to see today. I ate my meals today. I sleep in a bed undisturbed tonight. We have already lost… what else is there to lose? What could be worse?*

Knowing that one has hit the absolute bottom could be freeing, a joyful liberation. For a while, there was only living or dying, and nothing else. People celebrated simply for being alive.

As for Xeno, the first time the humans clapped eyes on him was to hear him say that he had stopped the carnage. That they were now going to be safe. He wore an excruciatingly beautiful human shell. The humans understood little of magic and sorcery and the raising of hellish troops. It was cognitively challenging to link that attractive face with the horrific carnage.

They lived, as promised, in a fairy tale world. The humans were fed, clothed, and sheltered. There was no need for work. The children, as was their wont, quickly started to play again. There was laughter, and songs, and togetherness. Some days, there was even ice cream.

No one came into Singapore and no one was allowed out. The airports were closed, seemingly for good. Passports became a farce. The humans' world shrank to fit the borders of a tiny island state. *But today, I am alive.*

Despite this, most humans of Singapore knew well enough not to trust Xeno. No paradise lasts forever, not least on earth. By and by, they began to wonder where Xeno obtained the food and provisions he distributed to them. Perhaps it was from the national emergency reserves? It was too good to be true. They would not last forever. What would he do when he had nothing more to give? Singapore could not survive being shut to the world, especially not as a small island nation surrounded by water, possessing no natural resources whatsoever. This much they knew for sure, at least.

~*~

Xeno had his pick of any of the most beautiful structures in Singapore to serve as his residence and command centre.

However, he chose to remain at Parliament House, mostly for sentimental reasons. It was where he had made his declaration of war. He had personally invaded it, as the symbolic act of taking up rule. It was where he had given his first media sound bite.

Besides, he was fond of the stern severity of the building. Singapore's past as a British colony was written into its architecture. He was pleased to take up the baton and work towards erasing the minor historical blip that was the past half-century. Independence did not suit the little island. He was determined to remedy that.

The first thing to be done was to acquire more land. Paradise on earth could not be the size of a peanut. And he planned to start with the lands that lay across from Singapore, separated merely by a small sliver of water.

"But there isn't enough fear," Xeno announced imperiously to a huddle of his oldest smoke demons. They were all seated in the assembly chamber of the Parliament House, playing at democracy. "I can feel our powers waning. We have killed so many humans that there are simply much fewer warm bodies now serving as conduits of fear to nourish us."

He cast a surveying glance at several of the reanimated corpses. They had become so bloated they were double their original sizes. Green blotches splayed across their skin. They leaked liquefied organs through their mouths and noses. Visible insects crawled gleefully all over the putrefaction. If Xeno possessed a sense of smell, it would have been impossible for him to sit so calmly in a hall crowded with so many corpses actively decomposing all at once. And of course, there were the damned maggots. They were a great nuisance; the cadavers leaked them in vast volumes as they shambled about obliviously. The floor was absolutely littered with them, transforming it into an outlandish pulsating alien landscape.

He sighed. "Get rid of them," he ordered his first lieutenants. "They're an affront to my aesthetics."

Without the cadavers supplementing his children of smoke, Xeno would have to strengthen his ranks before planning for outward expansion beyond Singapore.

He needed more fear.

~*~

The campaign started three weeks after Xeno's occupation first began. Individual humans started disappearing from their families overnight. People woke up in the morning, and someone was gone. Vanished without a trace.

"The door was locked. The main door was locked too. They were still locked when I got out of bed," Jonas's mother sat at her dining table, her head in her hands. "It's been a whole day since he disappeared and nobody has seen him."

Jonas was Leonard's assigned buddy back in Tekong. Leonard had finally vacated the crumbling building where he last held Marie Rose in his arms, and accepted Jonas's invitation to live with him and his family. During such times, it was not safe to be alone.

Jonas's father had gone missing in the night. Jonas's mother had simply woken up to an empty bed. There was no sign of struggle, no forced entry, no missing items from the house, no physical trace that anything had happened. Neighbours reported similar cases: a sister, a wife, a grandfather, a toddler. Yet, there was no discernible pattern to the disappearances. None of them were likely to have left the residences in the dead of the night. They all feared the return of the smoke demons and the walking dead.

Fraught days passed, and the missing did not return. There were no signs or clues as to where they could have gone, how they could have been kidnapped, and if so, *why* they had been kidnapped. There was no longer any conceivable reason for kidnappings to occur. None of the humans left in Singapore possessed wealth any longer. Luxury items and status symbols of the past lost their value entirely. Banknotes were worthless. The market economy of Singapore had collapsed. All living necessities were standard issue, courtesy of the new authority in town. People lived one day at a time, and were grateful to wake up the next. No one had any more than anyone else. All were equal.

The internet and mobile service providers had buckled even before the end of the first week of formal occupation. There were no telephone services. There were no postal services. After Xeno's first and only address to the country, the broadcast services slowly but surely collapsed as well. No one returned to work at the public transportation service providers. Why operate a train, captain a bus, drive a taxi cab when money was now worthless? Life in Singapore rolled right back to the pre-Industrial ages. Constrained by physical distance once more, people clustered in village-sized precincts. The food and supply rationing points became the only hubs of human activity.

As such, the very idea of kidnapping was ludicrous; it was as much an anachronistic relic of their former lives as were credit cards, bank accounts, Lamborghinis, Hypebeast sneakers, and Supreme T-shirts.

"It could not be a human doing this. It's Xeno," Leonard said bitterly. "It's psychological terrorism."

And so it was. No one knew when a loved one would be snatched away into thin air, never to return again. No one was able to find out where their missing loved ones had gone, or if they were coming back. No one could do anything, *anything*, to even try to save the ones they loved. There was nothing but despair, dread, worry, and fear.

10

SOLIDARITY, FAITH, AND LOVE

The days and weeks darted by like the flutter of koi in an ornamental pond. Fear boiled and simmered, a common undercurrent that flowed throughout the fragmented and disconnected human precincts.

Then, something broke.

Perhaps it was a fundamental law of nature that an organism could take only so much terror before it gives way to defiance. Perhaps it was the ancient Chinese principle of *yin* and *yang*, that when something reaches its apex, it inevitably transforms into its opposite. Perhaps it was the simple fact that a cornered animal had nothing more to lose.

Jonas did not mourn his father. He raged. Day after day, his anger seethed beneath the surface, roiling, churning, bubbling. Leonard could sense his friend's torment. Jonas had been close to his father. He was the kind of father who, when Jonas turned fifteen, had given his son his first sip of wine, beer, brandy, whiskey, and gin, so Jonas would not satisfy his curiosity elsewhere. He had bought Jonas a pack of cigarettes and, in a most matter-of-fact manner, explained to him why young men felt compelled to smoke and what would inevitably fester in his body if he kept the habit up. He shared the story—to Jonas's great embarrassment—of his first sexual experience, what it meant to most men, what it meant to most women, and the shades of grey in between. As an old man he touched no drink nor cigarette, but he was jolly as the day was long and he loved his family above all else.

Jonas had worshipped his father, in his own sullen adolescent manner. And he was determined to get him back.

The young men of Leonard's precinct gathered every Friday evening in Jonas's apartment. They had taken it upon themselves to oversee precinct matters best suited for the attention of fine young men—peacekeeping, security, mediation of conflicts, and the occasional requests to manoeuvre heavy objects.

They had had enough of Xeno's reign of psychological terror.

"It's been three weeks since my father disappeared," Jonas said to the meeting. "I know for a fact that he would *never* willingly abandon our family. This must be the work of Xeno."

One of the men, Xiang Hao, was generally reserved and quiet during meetings. This time, he spoke, trembling.

"They took my sister. Last night," he said simply, his face ashen and still. "My little sister. She's only seven years old. She…"

Xiang Hao stopped. He stuffed his face into the crook of his elbow for a moment. He was shaking, but he did not want the rest to see him cry. He allowed himself a few minutes to let the feeling pass and composed himself. The other men waited gravely.

"She is such a big girl already. But she still needs her *chou chou* to fall asleep at night," Xiang Hao fished out a baby pillow that he had stuffed in his pocket. Looking at the small well-loved pillow in his coarse brown hand, his tears welled again.

"I'm going to go get her back," Xiang Hao said suddenly, savagely. He brusquely dashed the tears from his eyes, impatient with himself for being emotional.

"Xiang Hao. Dude. What are you going to do, walk from Pasir Ris to Parliament House, knock on the door, and ask for Xeno? Demand for him to give your sister back to you?" someone asked.

"Yes," Xiang Hao replied. "Yes, that is exactly what I'm going to do."

There was a sharp silence. No one dared to mention the most pertinent fact that his sister might not even be still alive. *Properly alive.*

"I'm going with you," Jonas broke the silence. "I'm going to get my father back."

There was another momentary pause. The meeting members regarded each other wearily.

"I'm going with you guys too," Leonard added.

"What the hell, I'm in. Let's all go. Heavens knows they need the support," another member chimed in.

"My motorcycle still has gas. I'll ride to the nearby precincts and gather their support. I'm sure they have lost people like we did," said another.

The small knot of men nodded. They were so tired of waiting around, of watching and doing nothing of consequence while their country was stolen from them.

We will preserve and protect
the honour and independence of our country
with our lives.

"There is no honour living like this," Jonas spat. "Cowering in fear from day to day, hiding like vermin, meekly accepting what is given to us. Xeno said, this country is mine, and we did nothing. Xeno said, I will give you all you need, and we queued up obediently. Now Xeno is saying, your lives mean nothing. You are slaves, under my yoke and chain. All I need do is to jerk a few strings, and you little human puppets will perform the *danse macabre* of terror and pitiful abjection. It's time we did something. It's time we say to him: "Fuck you. We are not fucking afraid.""

The young men roared in assent.

~*~

The word spread quickly in Leonard's precinct. The people agreed with the young men; they no longer wished to cower and scurry as their loved ones were stolen from them one by one beneath the shroud of darkness and secrecy. They were tired of being afraid. They wanted answers. And they were going to join Xiang Hao and Jonas and Leonard and the young men of their precinct in their march for answers. They needed and deserved to know; they simply could not go on otherwise.

It was a cloudless day when the group of a thousand or so residents embarked on the seventeen-kilometre march from Pasir Ris to the Parliament House of Singapore.

They had kitted themselves out with food, water, and supplies as best as they could with their meagre belongings. Some of them carried improvised weapons, but many did not bother. The old ghosts and monsters were gone. The humans were on their own now.

A miraculous thing happened.

As the group passed through Tampines, and then Bedok, and then Ubi, and then Eunos, through to Geylang, Kallang, and Bugis, humans of Singapore started pouring out of their precincts and proceeded to join the group like ants dashing towards a pool of honey. The group grew larger and larger, becoming a crowd, then a pack, then a mass, then a horde. Motorcycles and cars with gas still in them sped around the island, spreading the news of the growing revolt.

The residents from the western, northern and southern portions of Singapore began marching towards Parliament

House from their own precincts. As the people hit Beach Road, they began chanting; dispersed at first, but their voices grew more and more strident as the infectious fever of the mob caught on.

"We're. Not. Afraid! We're. Not. Afraid!" the throng shouted with one voice.

Leonard and Jonas found themselves swept somewhere to the middle of the groundswell, surrounded by humans on every side. The crowd extended as far as the eye could see. They walked on either side of Xiang Hao, arms linked. Xiang Hao had stuck his sister's *chou chou* in his front pocket. They saw that many people carried portraits of their missing loved ones, holding them straight in front of their chests, facing outward so everyone could see the one they grieved. There were photographs of men and women both young and old, children of all ages, and even babies. The grief of the crowd ran deep, a strong undertow that carried them inexorably towards Parliament House.

"We're. Not. Afraid! We're. Not. Afraid!"

The pack passed the War Memorial Park, the pair of white chopsticks shooting towards the sky. The deserted skyscrapers of the Central Business District crowded in the distance like joss sticks.

Some people wept. They had not stepped foot in central Singapore for a while now. Memories of their former lives came flooding back, prompted by the icons of the Singapore glamour now lost to them. The jutting panes of the Esplanade Theatres, mimicking Singapore's unofficial national fruit.

The proud luxury hotels. The Victorian-era cathedrals. The museums. The shopping malls.

And then, City Hall. The Supreme Court and the Victoria Theatre came into sight. Parliament House came into sight.

The humans of Singapore linked arms. Family connected to family, stranger connected to stranger. No, in that moment, there were no strangers. All were family. All had grieved, scrabbled at life's tethers, and then been forced to grieve anew. All were one, equal beneath the sky's impassive gaze.

They marched toward Parliament House.

A distant figure on a horse had appeared in front of the square foyer. He was surrounded by a wall of troops guarding the entrances. The smoke demons.

As the first people spotted him, a new chant emerged and swept quickly to the ends of the crowd.

"Give. Them. Back!" the people shouted. "Give. Them. Back!"

Xeno furrowed his brow at the humans coming closer and closer to him.

He started laughing, laughing so hard that he snorted. Although he held no microphone, his laugh boomed and carried to every last person marching on Parliament House.

There was a short pause as people started at the unexpected sound. It was extremely loud for someone standing so far away from them. Xeno continued his madman's laugh, shrill and hysterical, as he surveyed the massive crowd surrounding the Parliament House.

"Give. Them. Back!" a lone voice from the crowd shouted.

The rest immediately took up the cue and resumed the chant. "Give. Them. Back! Give. Them. Back! Give. Them. Back! Give. Them. Back!"

The crowd had started moving forward, arms still linked. The earliest row of humans had reached the Parliament House's first entrance, a space between two rectangular gray columns. There were smoke demons guarding it. The humans stared down the monsters, unblinking. People held up the photographs of their missing loved ones like protest signs. In the midst of the massive throng, Xiang Hao held his sister's *chou chou* aloft. He was flanked by Leonard and Jonas.

"There is nothing to give. They are all dead," Xeno said matter-of-factly. His voice boomed as though there were speakers mounted in the sky. He looked directly into the crowd, his face expressionless. He held himself so gracefully atop his horse.

An animalistic cry arose from the crowd all at once, a cross between anguish and sorrow. It quickly turned into fury. The humans advanced on Parliament House.

People marched right onto the green grass lawns, on which Xeno had made his declaration of war an eternity ago. The smoke demons guarding the colonnades pounced on the first few rows of marching humans. Many went down, jostled to the ground by sharp claws. The horde continued to advance, still arm in arm. Its momentum was unstoppable. There was no way of turning back. No one attempted to—

it would have felt like attempting to swim upstream in a torrential river.

If there was an obstacle, the crowd surged around it. If there were smoke demons, they rushed right at them, meaning to trample them with the sheer force of their numbers.

All this while, the people shouted with a single voice: "We're. Not. Afraid! We're. Not. Afraid! We're. Not. Afraid! We're. Not. Afraid!"

Like water rushing over a broken dam, the crowd gushed into the compounds of Parliament House. They crushed the defending smoke demons underfoot. The smoke demons writhed amidst the stampede, unable to rise into form, as endless pairs of feet stomped over them. Amazingly, as the hypnotic chant grew louder and more defiant, the smoke demons became less and less substantial. They started to fade.

And all of a sudden, the humans were able to walk right through the smoke demons, as though they were merely projected holograms.

At that, the humans started to run.

They let go of one another and charged as a single phalanx straight toward the foyer of Parliament House. Their target was the lone figure atop his black horse, staring right at them unflinchingly.

The mob reached Xeno.

They had plunged right through the platoon of smoke demons arrayed before him. Grasping hands reached out, too many to count. They pulled him off the horse.

Xeno was swallowed whole by the voracious crowd.

It was a feeding frenzy. The improvised weapons came out. People yelled with crazed bloodlust and shoved each other to get to him.

The weaker had fallen over and were at great risk of getting trampled to death in the pandemonium. Leonard and his friends could barely see what was happening from their poor vantage points. All they heard were the anguished hollering of the people as a group of them bashed at a figure on the ground with their knives, hammers, rods, and assorted objects of all shapes and sizes. They could, however, see the humans being pushed and dragged to the ground in the confusion, crying out shrilly for help.

"Link arms! Link arms!" Leonard bellowed from somewhere in the midst of the mayhem.

Jonas, Xiang Hao, and the other young men from his precinct took up his call.

"Link arms! LINK ARMS!" they yelled.

Emphatically, they took up one another's arms and forced everyone in their immediate vicinity to do the same. People who had fallen over dazedly found hands stretching out toward them and hauling them back on their feet. An undulation ran through the crowd; it looked for all the world like the wind caressing a field of *lalang*. Hand reached for hand, one after the other. The ripple began from somewhere in the middle of the crowd and radiated outward. Toppled people were righted. People stopped jostling one another. For a moment, the crowd stood cheek by jowl, swaying.

Meanwhile, the head of the crowd busily swarmed Xeno in a flurry of activity. A man had fished out black cable ties from his pack. A group worked in methodical lockstep to secure Xeno's wrists and ankles with the cable ties. Throughout the commotion, Xeno laughed heartily, unfazed. His display of indifferent mirth unnerved and angered the people. Men rushed forward and kicked him wherever they could reach. Blows landed on his gut, his back, his shins, his head.

"Go on, let it all out! Let out who you *really* are!" Xeno taunted.

He shrieked with hilarity, rolling on the ground like a child being tickled. The cable ties were drawing blood.

The humans grew pale with fury. They ripped at his clothes, raining blows upon his bare flesh. All manner of objects were used as makeshift whips, flaying any exposed surface. Angry red welts brimmed as the skin started to split beneath the relentless thrashing. The mob's violence heightened with every peal of laughter.

A man knelt next to Xeno's curled, mutilated body. He wrenched Xeno's head back roughly, exposing his neck.

"Vampire," he snarled and spat in Xeno's face.

A lone roar surged and the crowd parted, expectorating another man who ran towards the pair on the ground. He gripped a long wooden broomstick, its end shaved into a sharp point.

Still yelling, the man charged and thrust the improvised spear into Xeno's chest, where a heart would be encased. There was a sickening squish as the stake penetrated flesh;

it was surprisingly less audible than anyone had expected.

"We created you, and now, we banish you!" the impaler proclaimed to all witnesses.

It was a grotesque sight. The long shaft of the makeshift spear stood rigidly, upright and unmoving, as the body it was embedded in remained convulsed in extreme jollity. Xeno was laughing so hard that tears ran down his face. He laughed so continuously, so uncontrollably, it seemed he was having a gelastic seizure. He twitched and clutched at his stomach. The laughter was compelling; it was almost hysterically infectious. Fighting the primal instinct to mirror another, the self-appointed leaders of the lynch mob clenched their jaws.

"Fire!" one hollered, as though attempting to summon it from the very heavens itself.

Matchboxes and lighters passed silently from hand to hand.

Meanwhile, Leonard, Jonas, and Xiang Hao had pushed their way to the front.

"No!" Leonard shouted. "Not this way. We are not like him. We are not savages. We will detain him and let him stand trial in a fair court."

"COURT!" the strongest of the lynch mob turned on him, spitting the word like a curse. "This is no man. This is a MONSTER!"

His face was engorged with the blood of vengeance. Veins stood out against his forehead like tributary rivers. Many in the crowd yelled in accord.

"Kill it by fire!" someone shrieked.

"Cut off its head!" another added.

The man who spoke to Leonard grinned slowly. "First, fire. Then, decapitation, to make sure."

His allied compatriots had received the various fire-starting tools from the crowd. Meticulously, they touched flame to fabric and set what remained of Xeno's clothing alight. Some smashed open the lighters and poured the fluid onto the incipient flames, stoking its progression.

The clothing caught fire very quickly. More and more flammable liquids were poured on the flames, sweeping it up into a hearty blaze in a heartbeat. It was incandescent, and terrible.

Xeno had pulled himself up into a seated lotus position. He was preternaturally still whilst the conflagration lapped and roared around him. The stake was still pierced through his chest. It wobbled slightly. Xeno himself was calm as a Buddhist monk performing the terrible and poignant deed of self-immolation.

The Zen master Thich Nhat Hanh had said: "The bodhisattva shone his light about him so that everyone could see as he could see, giving them the opportunity to see the deathless nature of the ultimate."

"NO!" Leonard yelled. "Not this way!"

With his friends by his side, he shoved the slack-jawed onlookers aside. He unearthed his 1.5-litre water bottle and poured the contents desperately onto the blazing body. Jonas and Xiang Hao followed suit.

Slowly, as if shaking themselves from their reverie, many others in the crowd began doing likewise. Bottles of drinking water appeared as precipitously as blinking fireflies. Dazedly, almost ritualistically, humans walked up to the seated Xeno and, turn by turn, splashed water on the flames consuming his body. The sporadic trickles mocked the roaring fire while it lavishly gushed smoke and heat. The fire had reached its zenith.

Nevertheless, more and more people stepped forward to dump the contents of their personal water bottles into the fire. The heat began to die down. The ground sizzled with steam and cooled. The dancing flames grew smaller and smaller. As the smoke cleared, the people could see what was left behind.

Nothing.

The people who were assaulting Xeno blinked. He had been seated on the ground just a moment ago, cross-legged and absurdly tranquil, partially obscured by smoke and flame. And now he was gone, as if he had never been. There was no sight of him anywhere. There were no smouldering embers, no ashes, no charred skeleton, no burnt fabric, nothing.

He was gone.

The people were stunned into silence for a long time.

Was he gone because they had burned him, or because they had saved him?

The humans did not dwell on the specifics. They had suffered for much too long. Abruptly, a cheer started up at the head of the mob, and the rest of the people began joining in with great gusto. There was much clapping, slapping of backs, vigorous hugging, kissing, and sobbing. The wave of jubilation crested and dipped throughout the crowd as people began breaking apart and spreading out for air.

The mob loosened and started to move. Many still circled the site of the fire in speechless disbelief. Nothing remained from the fire, not even the wooden broomstick that was plunged into Xeno's heart. The ground upon which Xeno sat was only slightly blackened with soot.

A small group had entered the Parliament House and clambered atop the peak of the building. They tore down the black flag and replaced it with a flag of Singapore unearthed from somewhere within the building. The stars and crescent once more fluttered against the azure sky. The responding ruckus was thunderous.

Leonard and Jonas hugged Xiang Hao, and Xiang Hao hugged his sister's *chou chou*. Despite themselves, they jumped up and down like a single many-headed, many-legged creature, yelling and crying at once.

High above their heads, the faint outlines of a suited man atop a galloping horse faded and faded as the wind carried it away. The man's lips were quirked into a small smile as he watched the celebrating crowd beneath him. He knew that in time, when the nation restored itself to its former likeness, when the fears that had birthed him swelled again, he would be called into existence once more.

~*~

It was a beautiful day on Pulau Tekong.

Leonard looked round at his freshly-minted sergeants. Their spines were straight as the grab poles on an MRT train. They wore carefully curated solemn expressions.

"So, gentlemen," he said to his team conversationally. "I must ask. Have you guys heard of the stories, of the mysterious female singing voice that can be heard past midnight in the third floor bunk toilets?"

"A… a ghost, you mean, Sir?" one of the sergeants stammered hesitantly.

Leonard lifted an eyebrow conspiratorially.

"Why yes… yes, I should think so. In my time, I saw her with my very own eyes. Let me tell you about her…"

The men talked.

Just beyond their field of vision, around the bends, between the edges of silent bunk and dark corridor…

A faint flicker of silken skirt.

AN INTERVIEW WITH YIHAN SIM

Why did you choose to present death and the afterlife in this way?

Admittedly, in *Fear of the Guest*, the subject of death is not extensively explored, except in a rather superficial and instrumental way to hold up the logic of this fantasy world where ghosts and spirits exist. In fact, the death of human beings per se is not addressed; human characters who died were turned into zombie soldiers in the army of The Guest.

As for the ghosts and spirits, their origins are deliberately left ambiguous. Is a ghost the leftover "essence" or "soul" of a previously living human? This is questioned by one of the characters, but left unresolved, so the reader is free to form his or her own theories about it.

The story also focuses more on the "death" of ghosts and spirits rather than that of human beings. This is depicted as a kind of fading away into non-existence, with a potential possibility of "revival" through storytelling and memory. Of course, this can be seen as a metaphor for the death that humans experience as well.

Did you set out to write this book with a specific end in mind?

When I started the story, the characters were very important to me. I wanted them to be vivid and captivating and special. I wanted to explore familiar Singaporean ghost stories from a different angle. As for the overall feel, I aimed for a tight, fast-paced story that is best classified as a contemporary fairy tale. I wanted it to be ambiguous and open to interpretation and discussion.

What are you afraid of?

In a way, *Fear of the Guest* is a laundry list of my own personal fears. Before I wrote this story, I was un-ironically and irrationally afraid of the creatures commonly depicted in ghost stories and horror movies in popular culture. Most sensible grown-ups do not literally believe in the existence of long-haired female ghosts *a la* Sadako. Yet, the scary imagery frightened me terribly, inexplicably.

Writing *Fear of the Guest* was therapeutic in some way, as I was then able to re-imagine and re-shape the spooky protagonists of ghost stories, turning them human-like and almost endearing. I walked a mile in hypothetical ghost shoes, tried to empathise with a ghost's point of view and gave them rational reasons for scaring us poor humans so.

More importantly, *Fear of the Guest* prominently contrasts the ultimately much more frightening adult fears we acquire as we grow out of childhood: the fears that are the uninvited guests in our lives—sudden illness, death, unemployment, mental disorder.

The character Leonard Liu's anxiety disorder—the fear that was turned on his own mind—was based on my own personal experiences. In the story, Marie Rose helps him find his way out of it. My hope is that people suffering from similar experiences of anxiety will take heart in the notion that this predicament can be overcome, if not, then sufficiently managed. And that it would require being open and vulnerable to receiving help from others (not necessarily supernatural).

Do you believe in evil – do you believe there is such a thing?

I recognise that the character The Guest almost appears on the surface precisely like a clichéd "evil" comic book character. But more fundamentally, he symbolises the deep-seated societal fears that pose a serious threat to human happiness and civilisation. There is also the related problem of whether might is right, whether The Guest is justified in his actions, whether means justify the ends. The story also challenges our entrenched anthropocentric presupposition that the value of human beings is always greater than that of any other creature. And yet, throughout the history of biological life, the strong has always prevailed. The human species would never have had the chance to dominate the earth, had the dinosaurs (who were the kings of the planet for over 150 million years) not been wiped out by a single chance astronomical event.

There is a running theory among philosophical circles that the concept of good and evil is created by mankind, and that all moral precepts are completely relative to the vagaries of time, place and culture. Yet, it also does seem at the same time intuitively uncomfortable to posit that because of this, anything goes, and we are never justified in denouncing anything as evil. I believe that we *are* justified in denouncing certain people or acts as morally blameworthy. The reasons for this would require much more delicate philosophical investigation which many esteemed academics have conducted much more sensitively and intelligently than I ever could and so I will not go further here.

ABOUT THE AUTHOR

Born and bred in Singapore, Yihan Sim loves animals, tattoos, storytelling, music, and most of all, her small hairy dachshund. She graduated from the National University of Singapore with a Bachelor of Arts with Honours in Philosophy. Her research interests include ancient Greek philosophy, classical Chinese philosophy and Zen Buddhist philosophy.

Fear of the Guest is her first novel.